"Are you asking me to take you to bed?"

Controlling her frustration and embarrassment with obvious difficulty, she told him, "To bed, to the couch, to the shower, on the floor. I don't care. Just take me away from this dark place I'm in. Unless there's someone else."

He was motionless for a long, agonizing moment. His features seemed set in stone.

"No."

"No, what?" The raw hurting in her voice forced his answer.

"Hell." He spoke the curse with a soft reverence, the words as gentle as the touch he brushed along the side of her cheek. "No one else."

She closed her eyes on a sigh and turned her head slightly to press her lips against his palm.

And he was lost. Damn the rules.

Dear Reader,

August in New York City is unique. The buildings and concrete seem to generate heat, people fan themselves on platforms while waiting for an air-conditioned subway car, and reading seems the best escape for the dog days of summer. This month, as I get lost in an Intimate Moments romance, my cat, Antoine, watches the ceiling fan go round and round. He may be contemplating a vertical leap, but I'm thinking how excited readers will be about August's lineup. What better way to spend a hot and muggy afternoon?

New York Times bestselling author Heather Graham returns to Intimate Moments with *Suspicious* (#1379). Set in the Florida Everglades, this roller-coaster read plunges us into a murder investigation…and an unforgettable romance between a detective and a hauntingly beautiful lawyer, who has a particular interest in these mysterious deaths. What happens when a woman wakes up to find she can't remember her identity but can speak several languages? Find out in veteran RaeAnne Thayne's *The Interpreter* (#1380), a love story that will keep you on the edge of your seat.

Vickie Taylor dazzles with her page-turning adventure *Her Last Defense* (#1381), involving a frantic search for a deadly virus-carrying monkey. As a doctor and a Texas Ranger try to ignore their fierce attraction, they plow through the forest to prevent a global crisis. In *Warrior Without Rules* (#1382), Nancy Gideon tells the story of a bodyguard who has his own way of dealing with life: Don't get too involved. Will his assignment to protect an heiress make him break his iron-clad code?

I wish you a joyous end of summer and hope you'll return next month to Intimate Moments, where your thirst for suspense and romance is sure to be satisfied. Happy reading!

Sincerely,

Patience Smith
Associate Senior Editor

Please address questions and book requests to:
Silhouette Reader Service
U.S.: 3010 Walden Ave., P.O. Box 1325, Buffalo, NY 14269
Canadian: P.O. Box 609, Fort Erie, Ont. L2A 5X3

NANCY GIDEON

Warrior Without Rules

Silhouette®

INTIMATE MOMENTS™

Published by Silhouette Books

America's Publisher of Contemporary Romance

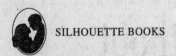 SILHOUETTE BOOKS

ISBN 0-373-27452-1

WARRIOR WITHOUT RULES

Copyright © 2005 by Nancy Gideon

Visit Silhouette Books at www.eHarlequin.com

Printed in U.S.A.

Books by Nancy Gideon

Silhouette Intimate Moments

For Mercy's Sake #648
Let Me Call You Sweetheart #851
Warrior Without a Cause #1350
Warrior Without Rules #1382

NANCY GIDEON

Portage, Michigan, author Nancy Gideon's writing career is as versatile as the romance market itself. Her books encompass genres from historicals and regencies to contemporaries and the paranormal. She's a *Romantic Times* "Career Achievement in Historical Adventure" and HOLT Medallion winner and has been on the Top Ten Waldenbooks series bestseller list. When not working on her latest plot twist at 4:00 a.m. when her writing day starts or setting depositions at her full-time job as a legal assistant, she's cheerleading her almost-independent sons' interests in filmmaking and R/C flying, or following NASCAR and picking out color schemes for the work-in-progress restoration of their 1938 Plymouth Coupe with her husband. And there's always time for a hot tub soak under the stars.

To my sister, Linda Dunn, for dragging me
from Michigan's cold winter to soak up the Ixtapa sun,
and for Terry and Marsha for help devising outlandish
plots, and Mike, with the romantic soul
for having tattoos worth their own story.

Prologue

She couldn't breathe.

The darkness was complete, shutting her away from the world. And from those who'd brought her to the damp, uncomfortable prison. How long? How long had she been in this void of sight, sound and sensation? When had she last heard movement above her?

Had they forgotten her? Had they left her here to die? *Daddy? Daddy, where are you? I want to go home.*

Terror clawed up her throat to strangle in a soundless sob. Duct tape sealed out the air just as it sealed in her screams. She tried to grab for precious oxygen only to gag on the cloth they'd shoved into her mouth. Like a swimmer going under, she thrashed against the ropes, against the cloth, frantically, futilely. She was drowning in the darkness. Panic beat inside her as she struggled to escape but the harder she fought, the more desperate her situation became.

There's plenty of air. Relax. Take it in slowly.

Gradually the fear subsided into a small whimper crouched in the back of her consciousness. She drew in thin streams of dank, life-giving oxygen through her nose.

He wouldn't let this happen. He wouldn't leave her here to die. All she had to do was be strong and stay alive.

She took another weak breath and the fright retreated once more. But for how long? How long could she hold on to the fragile hope that rescue would come?

Tears dampened the rough cloth they'd taped across her eyes. She fought them back as fiercely as she fought the hands that snatched her into the panel truck…how many hours, days ago?

Remember. Try to remember. Remember everything so they can catch these criminals and her father could bring them to an ugly justice.

The truck was green. The logo on the sliding doors had been rubbed out, leaving a smear of faded undercoating. She'd paid it no more attention than any of the other vehicles that had passed by until it had slowed and the cargo door had slid open. One minute she'd been standing in line outside the trendy London club, moving with the techno beat, excited to be using her of-age ID for the first time, and the next she'd been jerked off her feet too quickly to cry out in alarm. She'd never seen their faces. Something rough had been pulled over her head. Her flailing hands and feet had quickly been bound. She had lain on the uncarpeted floor of the vehicle, smelling gas and soil and tasting her own fear.

How long had they driven? She couldn't tell. Terror had robbed her of time and place and nearly of sanity. The roads had gone from smooth and straight to bumpy and full of twists and turns. And finally, they'd stopped. She'd had to pee. The pressure had built into an agony almost greater than her alarm. They'd sat her up, two sets of hard, hurtful hands. The sack had then been yanked off her head. As she'd blinked blindly against the sear of brightness, she'd heard the rasp of duct tape. She'd opened her mouth to scream for help, hoping there would be someone who might hear her?

Help me!

A wadding of cloth had choked back her plea. She'd bitten down, grabbing flesh and bone, grinding until the taste of blood had brought a savage satisfaction. A startled shout and a stunning dazzle of pain had burst inside her head ending that fleeting sense of victory.

The rest had been a blur. Her mouth and eyes had been taped shut, stifling her cries, stealing her sight, sending her into a emptiness so complete, an isolation so deep, it was like death. She'd been carried down, down. The temperature had dropped to a chill against her skin and after an hour or so it had seeped up from the dirt beneath her to permeate her very bones.

They'd left her.

For the longest time, she'd wept in soundless, nearly mindless anguish. Her fear had finally grabbed on to a narrow ledge of clear thought. Then anger.

How could they do this to her? Didn't they know who her father was?

Of course they did. Why else would she be here?

She dragged herself up off the hard-packed earth to lean back against rough stones, quaking with cold. Even as thirst and hunger and desolation chiseled away at her composure, one truth still held them at bay.

They didn't really know her father or they wouldn't have dared take her.

She dozed in brief snatches. In the total blackness, sometimes it was hard to tell if she was awake or asleep. Sleep was better, providing a respite from her misery. The dull ache in her bladder became a merciless roar and finally, awfully, she stopped fighting against it. She wept again, stopping only when her body had no more fluids to spare. She could hear her father's voice.

Crying about it never solved anything.

Daddy, help me! I won't cry anymore.

The simple act of drawing a breath scratched along the raw lining of her throat. She could no longer swallow and the very real threat of choking on her gag kept her fighting for that tenuous hold on reality. *Take slow, shallow breaths.* Just enough to survive until her father came for her.

And when he did, they would be sorry.

She sat up away from the wall. Her cramped muscles shrieked in protest.

What was that?

She strained to catch the sound again.

There. Footsteps overhead. Friend or foe? Rescuer or executioner?

Whimpers pushed against the gag.

A door opened. Footsteps, one set, started down, coming for her. Slow, heavy steps. Not the hurried sound of liberation.

She pressed back against the cut of stone, her body jerking in uncontrolled spasms as she waited helplessly to learn her fate.

She heard breathing, almost as harsh as her own. Then

pacing, agitated movements that kindled her own massing fear. A curse. Another. Guttural explosions of fury and frustration.

And then he spoke to her. None of them had spoken to her before.

"That son of a bitch. His own daughter. Can you believe he wouldn't pay a penny to save his own kid?"

A terror like nothing before it rose in a wave. Powering the surging fright was a tidal force of truth. A truth too terrible to contain.

He wasn't going to pay her ransom.

His money was worth more than her life.

Chapter 1

A lone figure moved down the hallway, slipping instinctively from shadow to shadow. He made no sound. It was
late. Those in the old building slept contentedly, unaware
of his passing. He might well have been a cloud drifting
across the cool gleam of the moon.

He paused, glancing behind him. He would have to re-
trace his steps to make sure he hadn't left a blood trail.
Later. For the moment he had only one goal, one destination, and it consumed him.

The key turned smoothly in the lock, admitting him into
the darkened room. The scent of furniture wax and fresh
herbs almost disguised the overall impression of emptiness. No one was home. No one had been home for a long
while.

He crossed the spacious living room without the benefit of light, heading with purpose toward the back of the

large third floor apartment. He moved like smoke, like pre-dawn fog, light, almost without substance, even as the toll of the past few months caught at him, threatening to drag him down. He couldn't afford to hesitate. Not yet.

He turned on one small light. It illuminated the mirror over a pedestal sink and the ghastly reflection it held, of hard features garishly detailed with traces of black and olive green paint. And smears of crimson. He wasted no time reacquainting himself with that grim mask. His attention turned to his right hand and the hasty wrap he'd bound about it. Slowly, he undid the saturated cloth and let it drop into the basin where it rapidly discolored the delicate porcelain. He moved his fingers, allowing a grimace. He'd need stitches.

Moving more gingerly now, with obvious difficulty, he undressed, letting his stale and stained garments remain where they hit the marble tiles. He'd pick them up later. Right now only one thing interested him. He reached to turn the water on full blast. When steam started to billow behind the circling curtain, he stepped over the high lip of the claw footed tub and into the merciless spray. A sigh escaped him.

He stood for countless seconds, letting the heat and force of the water beat the tension and achiness of abuse from his body as it washed the remaining face paint and blood—some of it his, some of it not—down the drain. Finally, because he knew if he didn't move, he'd be sleeping on his feet, he reached for the fine milled French soap and began to scrub away the layers of jungle soil and sweat. The pleasure was indescribable. At last, when he felt close to human again, he rinsed off in an icy sluice.

Even though he was physically ready to collapse on his

wonderfully forgiving Egyptian cotton sheets, he wasn't finished yet. He had calls to make, a report to write. Mental miles to go before he could sleep. And then he would sleep for days.

Standing naked in the kind glow of the bathroom light, he carefully attended his wounded hand. After the biting sting of antiseptic, he stuck on a couple of butterfly adhesives to hold the edges of the gash together, applied a sterile pad and mummified the damage with gauze. Tomorrow it would hurt as if the teeth of hell were chewing on it but he was philosophical about the pain. Better his palm than his throat. He dry swallowed several pain killers, purposefully not meeting the eyes in the mirror.

It had been a bad past few months. He'd almost forgotten the delights of becoming civilized once again. He pulled on his silk pajama bottoms, enjoying the feel of them against his skin after wearing the same rough, filthy fatigues until they obtained enough personality of their own to demand a seat next to him on the aircraft home. Home, where civilization and the finer things of life awaited him. Where he would decompress and forget the past weeks as if they never happened. No one really wanted the details anyway, just the results. His success rate was nearly untarnished. Which was why his phone wouldn't remain silent for long. He'd soak up as many pampering luxuries as he could before the next call would send him who knows where, but he knew it wouldn't be pleasant or remotely civilized. Terrorists were bloody inconvenient that way.

Switching off the light, he padded barefooted toward his front room via the kitchen, hauling his weariness behind him like Jacob Marley's chains. Scrooge that he was, he'd managed to miss Christmas again. One of the calls he had to make was to his mother, who knew better than to expect him but did, anyway. She wouldn't complain. She'd tell him he could make it up to her. She already held more markers than a loan shark. But she wouldn't complain. She knew why he did what he did. Sometimes that made her graciousness all the harder to bear.

Lights from the surrounding city created a soft pallet of colors upon his parquet floor. He loved the view at night, when mankind slept and the solid, unchanging history of the place seemed to come alive. Maybe he'd just sit awhile and soak up the peaceful ambiance. Maybe—

His gaze narrowed and flashed about the dark front room even as he deftly snagged a thin-bladed boning knife. Without breaking his stride, he continued toward the living room, his step light and now lethal, his body becoming a coil of deadly force.

"Tough night?"

Recognizing the voice from the shadows, Zachary Russell let the air rush from his lungs in a puff of relief. "Tough decade." He set the knife on the counter. "You took a chance popping up unexpected. How did you know I'd be here?"

"I know people who know people."

Zach advanced into the cavernous room. As his eyes adjusted to the dimness, he could make out the figure of his friend, Jack Chaney, seated in the deepest shadows near the window. That Jack had been inside his rooms without him sensing it was a testimony to his exhaustion. Of course, he could count the number of men on one hand with skills of his friend's caliber. He was one of them.

"Come all the way from the States for some of my coffee, did you?" Zach asked.

"If you were making some. Just black. None of that steamed milk or fancy flavored stuff, Russ."

"You Yanks are so plebeian in your tastes," he said, quirking his lip at Jack's nickname.

"We're just simple folks."

Zach switched on the light in his huge gourmet kitchen. It was the reason he kept the massively overpriced rooms he so seldom saw. He replaced the knife in the block and set about brewing a fresh grind of beans. The routine gestures and familiar smells were a salve to his battered soul.

It was always good to see Jack. They'd been best mates since his early days in British Intelligence. Jack was a straight shooter in their knife-in-the-back, cloak and dagger world. He'd secretly cheered when he heard of his friend's retirement. Not many of them actually got the chance to walk away from what they did, from what they were. Jack had a marvelous little wife back in the Midwest, a toughly independent lawyer he'd met while protecting her life, and together they were reforging a future that, frankly, Zach envied. Together, they'd started their own business, an elite bodyguard training center called Personal Protection Professionals. Jack had presented a card to him with a flourish and an open invitation. Any time he wanted to pick up some freelance work. Zach had the card tacked up on his board and smiled whenever he looked at it. Good for you, Jacky Boy.

As good as it was to see Jack Chaney, he didn't think for a moment that it was a social call. Jack wouldn't have come across an ocean just to say he'd been in the neighborhood and thought he'd drop by. And after the brutal toll his last mission had taken, he wasn't sure he was up for whatever Jack had in mind.

He carried the cups into the living room, knowing he'd soon find out.

"Coffee. Black and simple."

"There's nothing simple about anything you do, Russ."

Taking that as a compliment, he settled into one of the lavishly padded chairs he preferred over the strictly Old World continental theme he retained for the rest of his rooms. This was where he came to relax, where he came to sink down deep and rest for a long, healing while. But Jack was here this time to disturb that process.

"What happened to your hand?"

"Occupational hazard. Perhaps I could impose on you to do some needlework for me."

"Wouldn't be the first time."

"I'd do it meself but I'm vain about having the seams even. It's a bugger to do left handed."

Jack nodded. "Whose blood were you wearing when you came in?"

"No one you know or would want to know."

"You look like twenty miles of extremely bad road."

"Forty, and I feel every kilometer."

"Ready to retire and start that restaurant?"

"Giving it serious thought." He grimaced, shifting his cup to his uninjured hand. "So, to what do I owe this visit?"

Bless him, Chaney was always one to cut to the chase.

"Victor Castillo."

Zach straightened, all vestiges of weariness erased by that bit of the past he preferred not to dwell upon. Victor Castillo was his one professional blemish.

Castillo. A man one didn't mess with. A harsh, uncompromising figure in the global marketplace. Born in a small, poverty-ridden Mexican village, he'd parlayed street smarts into a personal dynasty worth millions in the States where they tended to ignore the gray areas of his business dealings. He'd repaid the debt by passing sensitive information to whatever agency would benefit…and would pay the most. He had no allegiance, no conscience, no scruples. And he'd collected a rogue's gallery of enemies who wanted revenge in the nastiest ways possible.

"And how is Victor?" He worked to keep his voice neutral but Jack saw right through him. His expression was half empathy, half regret.

"He sent me to call in a favor."

Instead of slumbering in his own bed, Zach spent the early-morning hours napping on an international flight. It was first class but it wasn't Egyptian cotton.

Chicago O'Hare was the expected press of humanity. Weary travelers shuffled from one terminal to the next, jumping out of the way for the beeping transport carts and nervously listening to warnings not to leave bags unattended. To Zach, it could have been any international airport in any city in any country. He'd spent so much time in the majority of them, he felt he'd earned a VIP spot at the baggage carousel.

As he stood scowling at the new scuff in the leather of his always packed bag, a hand reached down to take the handle.

"I'll get that for you, Mr. Russell."

He straightened, allowing the young Hispanic man to hoist his suitcase and garment bag.

"My name is Tomas. If you'll follow me, sir, transportation is waiting."

If the young man hadn't turned away so quickly, Zach would have been warned by his small smile.

The Chicago chill cut to the bone as he stepped outside the terminal. But there was no cushy limo waiting in the passenger pick up area to carry him in style to the Castillo estate on Lake Shore Drive.

A late-model sedan sat parked on the far side of the multiple traffic lanes. The trunk lifted expectantly in answer to Tomas's signal. As his driver started across the road ahead of him, the deep throated roar of a high-performance engine distracted Zach. He dodged back for the safety of the sidewalk as a motorcycle cut between him and Tomas. The young man never looked back, flinging the luggage into the trunk before starting around toward the driver's door. Only then did he grin, a brief flash of brilliant amusement, before ducking into the vehicle.

The rev of the bike's motor drew Zach's attention from his rapidly disappearing wardrobe. He hadn't even gotten the plate number. Swallowing down the indignity of falling such easy prey to an airport scam, he glared at the leather-clad rider who stood balancing the big growling machine between the spraddle of long, long legs.

Unforgettably gorgeous long legs skinned in black, tapering down to silver-tipped boots with three-inch heels.

The dark full-face visor was pushed up. Bold blue eyes regarded him with a challenging fierceness.

Ten years ago she'd been a vivaciously pretty seventeen-year-old and already modeling for her mother's athletic wear company. Now Antonia Castillo was heart-stopping. The recent picture in the dossier he'd studied on the plane was from the latest running shoe campaign, depicting Antonia crouching low as she exploded from starting blocks on a cinder track. Her body was an inspiration to would-be wearers of the shoes, long, lean, strong and bronze. The skimpy swatches of silk she wore left sleek legs bare and clung to her stupendous breasts. The photographer caught the essence of competition in her intensely focused expression. Thick dark hair was twisted back in a heavy braid revealing the bold angles of her face glorified in a sheen of healthy sweat. Those startling blue eyes against a deep skin tone gleamed with the spirit of personal challenge. Full, lusty lips peeled back from white teeth bared in a high-energy smile. Hell, it made him want to buy shoes.

And then he'd remembered how she'd looked the last time he'd seen her. Stripped of power, bereft of pride.

That was the face that haunted his nights.

Promise me. Promise me you won't say anything.

There was no trace of that vulnerable girl in the assessing gaze that swept over him now.

"You're looking well, Russell."

"A sight for sore eyes?"

Those dazzling eyes narrowed. Her tone chilled. "Once, perhaps."

Still, that greedy detailing had already told him.

Things were going to get complicated.

"Your father sent you alone to pick me up?"

The chin guard on the helmet hoisted an arrogant notch. "I pick up whom I please these days."

"To the delight of the tabloids, I might add."

"You've been keeping track of me." It was hard to tell by her voice if that notion annoyed or flattered her.

"You're hard to miss. Safaris, mountain climbing, sky diving, bunji jumping, a true media darling. A poster child for daredevils."

· And she made fine posters. He didn't have a lot of time to keep up with current events, let alone the social swirl, but Antonia Castillo was news. She wasn't found on the society pages at glittering events but rather in the pits at a race track, hanging with bikers or fight promoters, tossing back brews with the boys. One would never guess there were shadows hidden behind that brilliant smile. A courageous woman or one with something desperate to prove? It didn't matter. Both were dangerous and made him nervous because of their unpredictability.

"I take on each day as if it was my last, Russell. You disapprove?"

"It's your life."

"Yes, it is, and I live it as I choose." She flung that at him like a challenge, but he wouldn't take it. He didn't dare.

"Good for you, Ms. Castillo," was his cool, distancing reply.

He couldn't see her face, just those expressive eyes. They blazed hotly. With passionate feeling. Those kind of emotions, whether anger or insult or something more, were the last things he meant to inspire in either of them. But they were there, simmering now as they had then, just below the surface. Dangerous and unpredictable.

He'd been naive to think this would be just another job.

"Your father's waiting for me. Should I start walking?"

His dismissing prompt dashed the heat from her stare. Her reply was equal in its disinterest. "Climb on. Or take a cab if you're afraid the ride might be too much for you."

He snagged the spare helmet off the sissy bar and drawled, "I can handle anything with wheels or estrogen."

The corners of her eyes crinkled. He could imagine her sassy smile. "Ummm. We'll see." She snapped down her visor and goosed the throttle impatiently.

Slipping on his sunglasses and the open fronted helmet, Zach swung a leg over the seat. Even as he touched the saddle, the bike lunged forward, forcing him to grab on or get thrown. With one hand clenched in the back of her jacket and the other working the helmet strap, Zach managed to find the foot pegs as Antonia Castillo slalomed between slower vehicles, leaning and weaving like a downhill racer.

He wasn't dressed for a winter ride. His wool pea coat didn't shed the cut of the wind the way her leathers did. His bare hands and face burned as they headed out into the open air of the freeway southbound toward the lakeshore. Behind dark glasses, his eyes watered and blurred. But even as he grimaced into the brunt of the elements, a part of him enjoyed the fierce whip of the February air and the freedom of flying down the road unencumbered by convictions. Antonia's laughter filtered back to him as if she felt his exhilaration and mocked him because of it. With hands resting firm and wide spread atop the curve of her hips, Zach leaned back to appreciate the irony of the trip.

What was he doing here, on his way to meet with a man who'd tried to destroy him, with his hands enjoying the feel of a woman who, even when little more than a child, had turned him inside out?

His simple intentions were about to go straight to a chaotic hell.

Once they left the open highway for more sheltered

suburban streets, neighborhoods went from large homes crowding the manicured boulevards to massive family compounds hidden behind high walls. He observed, not as a casual visitor, but as a potential protector, noting side streets, surveillance opportunities, and possible danger spots until they reached the Castillo's residence.

The walls and iron gates were a newer addition, as were the video cameras. Nothing like being proven vulnerable to encourage an escalation in security. They idled outside the gates for less than eight seconds before the way parted, so obviously someone was on the job.

The house wasn't visible from the street. A long drive made of brick and cobblestone wound through a thick stand of oaks and firs shielding the residence from view. Not a good scenario. It provided too many places for an undesirable to conceal himself. Zach liked wide open spaces. He liked to see an enemy coming.

And that's how he felt as they took the final turn and he saw Victor Castillo, himself, standing on the front steps of his palatial kingdom.

The house was magnificent. Set on a bluff overlooking the slated waters of Lake Michigan, the sprawling three story stone and timber structure with its turrets, leaded glass and steeply pitched tiled roof reminded him of the estates that dotted the English North country. Though quaint in comparison to the true palaces of Europe, it made a statement of comfortable wealth and American arrogance. Much like its owner.

The last and only time he'd been here, he'd arrived in an unmarked panel truck with a cluster of other highly trained, highly motivated fellows. He went unnoticed, like the invisible working class meant to serve without intrusion. His job was to not garner individual attention from those in residence. This time, he'd been invited. So why was he wishing for that anonymity again?

He climbed off the back of the bike, moving cautiously until he was certain he had proper circulation in his legs. Antonia swung off and strode up and into the house without a word to him or her father. Why had she come to meet him herself if she was angry he was here? The number of questions piling up made him uneasy.

"Mr. Russell, you're prompt."

Unfastening the helmet straps with frozen fingers gave Zach an opportunity to observe his host. Castillo was a bit greyer at the temples, a bit thicker at the middle but he cut no less an impressive and inherently dangerous figure. He looked more like a drug lord thug than an international businessman. Or maybe that's because Zach knew his history. Blunt workingman's fingers tapped impatiently upon the weave of his Italian made slacks but Castillo was more than merely restless with the wait. Zach could sense his uncertainty and nervousness. Not much worried someone of Castillo's stature, a man who had an entourage paid to fret over details for him. So that meant whatever reason he had for summoning someone for whom he had no respect was personal and threatening enough to want someone outside his organization. Why else would he be standing outside in the cold to greet the man he'd once tried to crush?

"I pride myself on punctuality. Shall we get to the point of your invitation?"

He saw it then, the intense dislike Castillo harbored for him. It passed briefly across his expression before he gestured to the front door.

Step into my parlor.

What was he up to?

The foyer of the Castillo estate was meant to impress with its massive scale. The vaulted ceiling soared overhead, revealing heavy beams and an impressive chandelier. The tiled floor, ornately carved woodwork and plastered walls all aspired to an Old World feel, but to Zach, who'd grown up steeped in that Old World tradition, the setting was like Castillo, an artificial facade of respectability imitating something it wasn't.

What was impressive was the vista spread out before him. From the foyer, several steps led down into the living room and a wall of windows capped by fanciful stained glass designs. The breathtaking view of the lake was unobstructed except for a sight even more amazing. The lithe, leather-clad figure of Antonia Castillo where she stood looking out upon that bleak winterscape. The four color photos hadn't done her justice. As a connoisseur of fine things, he knew a masterpiece when he beheld one. And she was a work of art.

Her dark hair hung down in a heavy braid, leaving her chiseled profile unencumbered. Hers was a lush, savage beauty like the lake beyond, all strong facial angles, slanting cat's eyes and those pillowy lips that pouted and provoked a man beyond reason. The leather glazed her long legs and fit her tight backside the way a man's palms itched to. She'd taken off the jacket. Beneath it, she wore a snug white top with thin spaghetti straps. Atop her sleek, willowy build, the bold, gravity-defying fullness of her breasts within that thin stretch of cotton knit was another marvel to behold. When she turned toward him, her chin notched up and her shoulders back, thrusting out her chest with all the challenge of twin nuclear warheads. Fascinating yet deadly.

Of course, she meant for him to look. What man could help himself? So he did, staring at that awe-inspiring bounty with a cool detachment of someone in an art gallery.

"Antonia," her father barked. "You're making a spectacle of yourself."

"I meant to, Father."

At least she was honest in her intentions.

"Put on something decent."

"Why?" she challenged with a higher tip of her chin. "Mr. Russell is hardly a guest. And it's nothing he hasn't seen before."

"Antonia!" Red-faced, Castillo turned to Zach. "I apologize for my daughter. She has no manners."

Zach remained carefully stoic. It wasn't his job to teach them to her.

Castillo glared at the defiant young woman. His tone was soft and furious. "Go make yourself presentable then join us in the study."

Realizing she had taken her point as far as she dared, Antonia pivoted on those high, high heels and swiftly stalked from the room.

"She forgets herself," came Castillo's almost weary apology. "She's had no one to control her since her mother died."

Zach waited impassively. Castillo wasn't interested in any comment he might make on his domestic situation. Finally, when the older man continued to gaze distractedly through the doorway his daughter had taken, Zach cleared his throat.

"Why am I here? Jack Chaney said you asked for me specifically. Why? I wasn't aware you held any particular fondness for me or my talents."

Castillo's stare cut through him like a surgeon's blade. "I don't. But unfortunately, my daughter does. She's the reason you're here. She seems to think you're the only one who can keep her alive."

Chapter 2

"There have been threats."

"To the family or to the business?" Zach asked as he settled into a stiff brocaded chair on the opposite side of Castillo's cluttered office desk. He noticed a photo of his wife and daughter, a nice black and white showing mother with preschool-aged child as well as a glamorous color portrait of Mercedes Castillo, but no recent picture of Antonia.

"Both."

"Any particular reason?"

Castillo frowned, taking Zach's nonchalant tone to mean there were so many, he could take his pick. "We're in negotiations to move Aletta's manufacturing and distribution plants to Mexico. The Union is trying to block the move, but what can they do?"

"Make threats?"

"Perhaps."

"How many workers will lose their jobs?"

"Among the five plants, about seven thousand. But they'll be given severance packages. It's not as if they're being thrown out onto the streets without warning."

"That's generous of you."

Castillo's expression tightened at the drawled sarcasm. "It's business. It's more than I'm required to do for them. I can't expect someone like you to understand the economic difficulties of staying competitive in the United States. The only feasible way to continue at a profit is to move production below the border."

"I'm sure the thought of a few million more a year for their summer homes motivated the board of directors to make that decision."

"It is *my* decision, at least until tomorrow night."

"And then?"

"And then," intruded a low female voice, "it becomes Antonia's."

Zach rose to greet the stunning woman who entered. Dressed in a severely tailored suit, she was tall, voluptuous and cold as ice, from her chilly tone to her glacial stare. He recognized but couldn't place her.

"Mr. Russell, do you remember Veta Chavez, Antonia's companion?"

The term companion threw him for a moment, then he recalled. "Your father was in charge of security."

"Yes. He's retired. I'm in charge of Antonia now."

He lifted a brow. "Not an enviable task."

She rebuked him with a haughty sniff. "Toni and I have been best friends since we were children. She's only difficult if she's provoked. Since your name was mentioned she's become increasingly difficult, so I must assume she finds you most provoking."

Zach merely smiled as he pulled out a chair for her. She settled gracefully, like a female panther. "So what happens tomorrow?"

"Toni turns twenty-eight and inherits controlling interest in Aletta."

"It was my wife's company," Castillo explained. "Her father established it, and she made it successful beyond his wildest expectations. She was an incredible business-woman. I had hoped Antonia…" He let that sentiment drift off on a sigh. "The company is hers tomorrow whether she is ready to assume control or not. I still retain a substantial holding, so she won't have full rein."

"And you fear someone might try to intimidate your daughter into keeping her company here in the States."

"That's a bit simplistic, Mr. Russell. No one can bully my daughter. She is absolutely fearless except for the one small vulnerability I had hoped would never be discovered beyond those in this room."

"But someone found out."

"Exactly, and they've been terrorizing her," Veta told him crisply. "She'll deny it, of course, and it may be noth-ing. I've given every assurance that I can handle things."

"But I won't take that risk," Castillo concluded. "I will not have my business jeopardized."

Zach's dislike for the man hardened into a disgust he could keep from his carefully schooled expression, but not from his wry comment. "And here I thought your concern was purely fatherly."

"Aletta is family, Mr. Russell."

Zach stood to offer Antonia Castillo his chair as she returned to the room. She'd changed from a liquid spill of leather to the soft, no less revealing drape of a sleeveless tunic over wide-leg pants of some fluid butter-colored material. Her braid was now secured to the back of her head in an elegant coronet and thin gold chains swung from her ears. The effect was as sensually feminine as the earlier had been in-your-face sexual. And he was not unaffected.

"What concerns Aletta impacts all of us," she continued, dropping carelessly into his seat.

Zach remained standing, leaning back against a bank of wooden file cabinets with arms crossed casually across his chest.

"Contrary to my father's opinion, I plan to do whatever necessary to assure its continued prosperity. I will not be swayed from that plan by someone playing cruel tricks in hopes that I'll fall to pieces."

"What kind of tricks?"

Though her features never lost their smooth hint of disdain, something flickered in her eyes.

"I can give you the details later if you decide to take the job. Or can I assume you already have since you're here?" Her tone was resigned and annoyed, but something in those eyes beseeched him on an unspoken and perhaps an unconscious level.

"I'm here because Jack Chaney asked me to come. As a favor to him, I'll listen to what you have to say, then I'll decide. I don't do civilian contract work as a rule."

He could see that unsettled her. She thought he'd come because she and her father had demanded it. His priorities took her arrogance down a notch. And then he again caught a glimmer of that raw vulnerability, of the frightened girl she'd been ten years ago when he'd first thrown back that door. He refused to let himself soften to that memory. She was not that girl anymore. He'd done his job then, and they'd almost cut the legs out from under his career by way of gratitude. This time, he'd be more cautious in his approach.

"Tomorrow night, I celebrate my business coming of age. The next, I fly to Mexico to go over the contracts transferring Aletta's production hub outside our borders. There'll be meetings and publicity and media. And protesters. I need someone to protect me," Antonia stated at last. How difficult that must have been for her.

"What you need is a team of about five men so that you're covered 24/7. You need a coordinated effort that one man can't provide. Surely, Chaney told you that. He has men available for that kind of thing."

"We don't want high-profile protection. We need discreet." She paused, looking uncomfortable with her next admission. "We asked for you because you know my past, and there'll be fewer explanations to be made. Mr. Chaney assured us that you were the very best available."

"I haven't said yet whether I was available. You haven't specified exactly what you want me to do."

"Become my shadow, and if needs be, a wall that will stand between me and any harm someone might think to do."

He said it before her father could. "You're very trusting, considering I failed you once before."

He hadn't expected her to take any responsibility for that and she didn't.

"I see you as a man who takes failure very personally. I believe you'll be motivated to make certain it never happens again." She threw it down as a challenge, daring him to pick it up. Knowing he would. But on his terms.

"How very right you are there, Ms. Castillo, which is why, if I take this job, it will be with your explicit agreement to follow my rules."

Her stunning blue eyes narrowed suspiciously. "Rules? My employees usually don't get to make the rules."

"This one does and if you fail to follow them to the letter, I will walk away without a second's hesitation regardless of the situation. Understood?"

Oh, yes. He could see she understood, his insistence and his reasoning. And she wanted to fling his demands back in his face with a shove it up your arse. Because she didn't, he began to see just how scared she really was.

"What are your rules?"

"Just three and they're very simple. Even a child can follow them." She bristled at that but said nothing. "Rule number one, I'm in charge. Everything concerning you goes through me and must be cleared by me."

Veta spoke up. "Victor, I can't allow that."

But Castillo put up his hand to halt her objection, allowing Zach to continue.

"Everything," he emphasized, his gaze never leaving Antonia's. "Nothing happens without my knowledge and consent. Clear?"

"Crystal" she replied frigidly.

"No interference. Not from your father, not from Ms. Chavez, not even from the police."

"Victor," Veta protested more vehemently. "Surely you can't agree to this nonsense."

Zach held the icy blue glare of the woman seated below him and very clearly summarized, "There's me and there's God." Jack had been fond of that particular saying, and Zach found it suitably dramatic to make his point. "You will only listen to me. And you will do exactly as I say. No questions, no arguments."

She was having trouble swallowing that one down but she did so long enough to ask, "And Rule Two?"

"Rule Two, where you go, I go. No exceptions. To the hairdresser, to your girls' night out, to your gynaecologist appointment. I'm right there."

"And when I shower, will you scrub my back?"

He allowed a faint smile at that brittle retort. "If you like. Privacy will be strictly at my discretion. And I can be very discreet." At that last assertion, he lowered his tone ever so slightly so she would catch the reference. She knew he could be and would be again.

"And Three?"

"Rule Three, nothing personal. This is strictly a business arrangement. I will not be played. I will not be drawn into your affairs, private, professional or otherwise. I won't allow anything to distract me from my job, so don't expect more than that."

"Heaven forbid that you be distracted." Her stare glittered like shards of glass.

"Those are the rules. No exceptions and no deviations. If you'll follow them, I'll keep you safe. Agreed?"

She stared up at him, pride warring with necessity. Each rule was a deeper intrusion, a sharper cut into her independence, a tighter rein of control into the intimate details of her life. But he hadn't created the situation she found herself in. If she wanted his help, this time she'd do it his way.

"I will follow your rules," she acquiesced at last. "No matter how overbearing and obnoxious I consider them to be."

He did smile then, a wide appreciative grin. "You're entitled to your opinion as long as I have your guarantee of cooperation."

"Would you like it written in blood or would a hand-shake do?"

She put out her hand in a forthright gesture that took him off guard. This spirit of acceptance was not what he expected. He took her hand gingerly. Her handshake was firm, assertive but gentle, too, because of the binding across his palm. She glanced at the wrapping, her brow furrowing, but she didn't ask questions. He liked that and the fact that with the confidence of her grip came the soft silken feel of her skin. And the moment he became aware of it, he pulled back.

Looking relieved that all had been concluded without verbal bloodshed, Castillo asked, "How much do you want?"

"To keep your daughter alive?" His jaw clenched tight to keep the rest unsaid. Would the son of a bitch come up with the cash this time or haggle for the best price?

"Name it. Whatever you want."

Castillo's money was the last thing Zach wanted. "Whatever Chaney charges is fine with me. He'll see I'm remunerated."

"I didn't think you worked for Chaney."

"You've just subcontracted my services through Personal Protection Professionals. They'll send the bill. Now, if you don't mind, I've had back-to-back transatlantic flights and would very much like to freshen up a bit before going over the particulars with Miss Castillo."

Antonia rose immediately. "I'll show you to your room. I'm sure Veta plans to launch quite an argument with my father once we're out of earshot."

Nodding to his host and the lovely Ms. Chavez, Zach followed Antonia into the hall, noting the Salome sway of fabric she put in motion with her brisk step. She walked like a prize fighter, with an arrogant strut, leading with her chin held high. And he found it more alluring than any practiced swivel.

"And will she win any points?"

Antonia glanced back at him. "Who?"

"Ms. Chavez."

"No." Sure, not smug. A woman who recognized her power but didn't gloat about it. "What did you do to your hand?"

The shift in subjects had him off balance again. He didn't like that, the feeling of having to catch himself to stop a fall. He'd always been that way around her. Just her. He made a quick note to widen his literal and his mental stance.

"Worried that it will handicap my efforts?"

Again, the curt, "No. Just curious. Or is that against the rules, too?"

"Just a cut. Nothing serious. How about you tell me how serious your trouble is?"

They'd reached the stairs, a massive column of heavily carved wood that rose up with two separate landings to an open rail above. The wall behind it was stained and leaded glass. He'd bet it was spectacular with the summer sun shining through it. But in the weak winter light there was barely enough illumination to see beyond the first turn of the deep red runner. He didn't like it—the dark paneled halls, the shadowed stairs.

"It's no secret that moving Aletta out of the country made a lot of influential people very angry. They'd be thrilled to see negotiations fall through—or at least be delayed if for some reason I was unable to competently handle them. A delay would give them more time to mount a legal defense or find attractive incentives to keep production in the States."

What was attractive was the way the supple knit clung to her hips and buttocks as she mounted the steps ahead of him.

Rule Three, Russell. Rule Three.

"What have they done to discourage you?"

She paused on the landing as if to catch her breath then started up once more. "Just basic intimidation at first, you know, rocks through windows, delightfully graphic graffiti, a chicken nailed to the front door."

"Of this house?" That shocked him. To get inside the perimeter implied a breach of security beyond the capabilities of a few disgruntled Union workers. It meant he was dealing with a professional. Or someone on the inside.

"That was about two months ago."

She fell silent, prompting him to conclude, "But it got worse."

"Do you know what a virtual kidnapping is?" She'd reached the hall and turned to face him. He stopped a few steps below and had to look up at her. Her features were taut as carved marble.

"It's a con. The scammer gathers information on a victim, waits until they're temporarily out of reach then calls their families to say their loved one has been snatched. If they're good and quick, they can have the money before the family realizes they never had their loved one at all. It's a nonviolent but emotionally brutal trick." His expression stilled. "Someone called your father."

"I was coming back from skiing in Colorado. I was involved in a minor car accident and missed my flight. Weather took out communications. Because of the holidays, there were no seats available on anything with wings. By the time I managed to charter a flight, they'd already made contact to say they had me. They demanded one point five million."

"Did he pay?" His question sounded as soft as a prayer in the cavernous stairwell.

"He said he wouldn't pay without proof that they had me."

Mesmerized by the fierce intensity in her face, Zach held back his curse.

"They sent him a ring I'd been wearing. I'd lost it several nights earlier. I thought I'd misplaced it. He sent them two hundred and fifty thousand and told them he wouldn't send a penny more. I arrived two days after the exchange. Imagine my surprise to find out what I'd missed."

Yeah, the fact that her father treated her like the blue light special at a discount store.

"Coincidence, do you think?" he asked at last.

"The kidnapping? Perhaps. If someone knew the details of the first, they'd know there wasn't a very good chance that they'd come out of it rich men." Her tone was remarkably free of bitterness.

"Unless it wasn't about the money."

"What, then?"

"Terror. Simple, stark terror. The quickest way to bring an enemy to its knees is with the idea of what could happen."

She had to be thinking about it. It had to be tearing at her, undercutting her sense of safety. For a moment, he was blind-sided by the memory of what he'd found in that room. But she betrayed none of that inner fright with her next bold words.

"My father's knees won't bend and neither will mine, not before empty threats and scare tactics."

"And if they become more than that?"

"Keep them from becoming more than that, Russell. That's why I hired you. My only rule—don't let them get close. Don't ever let them get close enough to touch me."

The briefest tremor shook through her voice, just a ripple to disturb the smooth surface calm.

Before he gave thought to it, he started to reach out to take her hand, thinking to extend a reassuring press. But when she caught the movement toward her, she took a rapid step back to place herself out of range. He let his hand fall back to his side and sought to console her with his sincerity instead.

"They will not get by me. My word on it."

She stood for a moment, gauging him for his ability to keep that solemn vow, strung tight as the piano wire that had nearly taken off his hand a few days earlier instead of his head. And gradually, she began to uncoil.

"Tomas put your bags on the third floor."

"Is that where you sleep?"

"No. My room's down there." She gestured toward the right, but her stare was still locked into his.

"And where do you want me?"

She gave a nervous little laugh. "I'd have you sleeping inside my pajamas with me if it didn't compromise Rule Three."

Visuals, hot and embarrassingly graphic, ran wild through his imagination, but he managed a thin smile.

"There'll be none of that. What are your plans for the next two hours?"

"I've got a photographer waiting for me. We're going to do some publicity stills."

"And who else will be there?"

"About a dozen hair, wardrobe and makeup artists, not to mention lighting specialists, the assistant and the assistant to the assistant and Veta. Just a few close personal friends. I don't leave home without them."

"Don't leave the house."

"I won't. Where will you be?"

"Unconscious for the next two hours. And then I'll be on the job."

Why hadn't she told him the significance of the ring?

Toni sat in the styling chair letting her thoughts free flow as she made herself malleable to those whose job it was to make her into a priceless marketing tool. On the magazine page, at least, her value was immeasurable.

She glanced down at the unique twist of precious metals she wore on her little finger. Would he remember it? More important, would he understand the implication of someone else knowing what it symbolized?

She should have told him. It was foolish to keep secrets from the one man who knew the worst of them.

His word. He'd given it to her ten years ago and hadn't broken it, not even at the risk of losing his job and his credibility. She would hold to his promise like a lifeline, for that's what it was. The one fragile strand tethering her at the precipice of panic and indecision. She could cling to his word as the one certainty in the chaos her world had become.

She stared at the illusion they'd created in the mirror. Strong, vital, fearless, feminine, the epitome of woman power. A sham. A mask she wore to hide the frightened little girl inside. She wore her reputation as a wild child like armor, deflecting those who would get close while keeping herself safe and yet a prisoner inside. Zachary Russell had freed her ten years ago, but in many ways, she was still a hostage.

Resentment for the situation created a lump of anger and anxiety wedging solidly in her throat, refusing to go up or down. She loathed having to call him, to beg through his friend that he return. Because seeing him was a reminder of what she was constantly trying to overcome. The fact that it had been her fault. The fact that despite all she had done, she was still vulnerable. His presence, his rules, the way he looked at her were all unspoken reminders of what he knew, of what he'd seen. Having him here was her private heaven and hell. He was the only one who could strip off the mask she wore and leave her naked and exposed. And he was the only one who could make her feel safe enough to do the things that lay ahead. So forge ahead, she would. Business as usual.

"Any time you're ready, Ms. Castillo."

Under the hot lights and strict direction of her photographer, Toni lost herself in her work for the next two hours. She allowed herself to become a posable mannequin, for her mask to be manipulated so she became any woman they wanted her to be—strong and dynamic, feminine and free-spirited, an aggressive warrior pursuing victory at any cost. It was easy to pretend to be someone else when there was nothing else inside her. Until she glanced up to see him standing in the shadows and, momentarily, the pretense fell away.

"Hold that look, Toni. That's perfect," her photographer cooed. "Now, give me more. Work with it. You're a woman yearning for something just out of reach. Let me see that longing. Let me feel it. Great, baby. That's it."

He'd changed into a pair of dark slacks and a cabled sweater, but there was nothing casual about his stance or his ever moving gaze. Ten years had passed and he still made her heart beat with a crazy, out-of-sync rhythm. She'd seen better looking men, men with the features of an Adonis who had feet of clay. It wasn't about perfection. That wasn't what made Zachary Russell so compelling.

To a critical eye, he was average in appearance, average height, average looks, nothing, at least outwardly, to set him apart. He wore his brown hair buzzed nearly to the scalp, perhaps in defiance of a receding hairline or maybe in indifference to it. His nose was crooked, his mouth too thin except when he unleashed an occasional and always surprisingly wide and white smile. He had nice eyes, intelligent, kind, she'd thought at first, and changeable the way hazel eyes had a tendency to be. And he had a jaw like granite, stubborn, often stubbled, squared and fitting a face on Mount Rushmore.

No, there was nothing spectacular about his features, just a pleasant arrangement that was not unappealing. What set Zachary Russell apart, what made her pulse skip and leap like a child's game of hopscotch, was the total package.

The man reeked of charisma. He had a way, with his direct gaze, of conveying an intensity, a strength, a confidence that both overwhelmed and reassured. His silky, accented voice held just the right amount of authority backed with reasonableness. His body language was all bold, male assertiveness with nothing to prove, no one to impress. But by heaven, he impressed her. Right from the start.

Ten years had passed. Time had been both kind and cruel. He still wore the same sleek air of sophistication the way he donned his expensive wardrobe. Casually, comfortably. There was still compassion in his gaze but also a ruthlessness that could suppress other more forgiving emotions. There was now a harshness in the angles of his face, making him more formidable than magnetic. And scars, she'd noticed, beneath his right eye and on his chin. To match the one he'd have on his hand. He'd been a consummate professional ten years ago. Whatever had transpired in that interim decade had made him into a deadly and decisive force. She wondered a bit guiltily how much of that change had been her fault. Now he was a man of narrow smiles that never reached his eyes, one of strict rules and unforgiving principles. One who'd allow no harmless flirtations.

The camera whirled, happily capturing her wistful expression. That look stiffened when she noticed Veta sizing up her security competition. Her friend crossed over to Russell, her movements contrived to seduce and conquer. Many a man had made the mistake of underestimating Veta Chavez. They saw only the lush body and alluring features and not the steel of the woman within. Zach gave her a brief glance, but true to his word, refused to be distracted. They spoke, whether of the job or of the past, Toni could only guess. All she knew was when Veta's red-tipped finger drew a line down the center of Zach's chest to gain his attention, she was drawing a different sort of battle boundary, one Toni couldn't cross. She could compete with her older companion in realms of business and social situations, but when the stakes took a turn toward the intimate, Toni was quick to cash in and back out.

"Toni, you lost it there."

Sensitivity to her moods was what made Bryce Tavish extraordinary behind the lens. He was temperamental but a genius at the same time, and Toni enjoyed working with him. They were friends as well as business professionals. "Shall we take a quick break? Rufus, there's enough glare off her skin to give me a sunburn."

While one of the makeup people touched up a shiny spot on her forehead, another one of the assistants approached with a flat mailer envelope. Without a second thought, she took it and tore open the end. Anything to distract her from the cozy conversation going on back in the shadows. There was a garment inside the envelope. A pullover top made of an electric blue spandex. Something from advertising, perhaps. But the sleeve was torn and there were rust stains on it. With a puzzled frown, she began to examine it more closely. Somehow, it looked familiar, like something she might have worn. There was a piece of paper tucked inside the neck line. She unfolded it and with the block printed words upon it, all else crumpled.

WHERE'S THE MONEY?

A sudden suffocating tightness closed about her throat. Her hands convulsed about the bright stretchy fabric.

She had worn it.

Those weren't rust stains.

She tried to draw a breath. The sound strangled in her chest. Over the engulfing roar in her ears she heard Zach Russell's harsh command.

"Get the bloody hell out of my way."

She tried to swallow and felt herself choke as if something was wedged in her airway. The package fell from her hands, the note fluttering from numbed fingers. An odor of dank earth and the sensation of cold preceded a swelling blackness so complete, she never felt Zach catch her on her way to the floor.

Chapter 3

Antonia Castillo sat on the windswept terrace oblivious to the outward temperature as she watched the white-capped waves below. The elements paralleled her mood, cold, agitated and forbidding. She didn't turn at the sound of familiar footsteps approaching from behind. For a long moment, Veta stood at her side without speaking. Finally, she asked the expected.

"Are you all right?"

"Sure, fine, peachy. I need a cigarette."

Veta passed over the contraband with a pack of matches and waited for Toni to struggle with the cutting wind to light it. After a deep draw, Toni stared in disgust at the shaky state of her hand. She wasn't fine. Nowhere close.

"Do you want one of your pills?"

That was Veta. No time wasted on sympathy or sentiment. Right to the practical solution.

"No, I do not want a pill," she snapped, denying the lure of that blanking peace of mind and spirit. "I need to be able to think. Where's Russell?"

"Reading the staff the riot act, I believe. A little late for that now, don't you think? Toni, we don't need him here. We can handle this in house."

That was her father talking. *Don't involve outsiders. Take out your own trash. Family business is family business.* She took another drag on the cigarette, letting its harshness distract from the bitter taste of those edicts.

Her voice was low and strung with steel. "I need him here, Veta. I don't expect you to understand or agree but I need to know that you're with me, too."

Veta was her strength. The role model she'd looked up to since she was a child, the savior who'd ended part of her nightmare with a single shot, the cooler head and constant support she'd needed to assume her mother's place. She was more than an assistant, more than her security, more than a friend, more than her advisor. If Toni had pressed her to put a name to their relationship, she would say with typical brevity, family.

Veta bent to loop her arms about Toni's shoulders in an uncharacteristic outward show of solidarity. The gesture wound about Toni's heart with equal warmth. "You know I am. Just the way it's always been. Whatever you want, Toni. I'll play nice. It's a big sandbox."

That coaxed a smile. And released a huge pent-up load of anxiety. She was not alone. Toni patted her friend's arm. "Thanks."

"Besides, someone needs to keep an eye on Russell to make sure he's doing his job. I can't say that I'm impressed so far."

Toni chuckled reluctantly. "Leave Russell to me. You watch my back."

She straightened and stepped to an impersonal distance. "He's all yours."

From the sudden chill in Veta's tone, Antonia guessed her companion's nemesis had finished dressing down her entourage and was coming to lecture her on the facts of life as dictated by Zachary Russell. She took another puff from Veta's imported cigarette and shot a fierce jet of smoke full steam ahead.

"So, what did you find out?" she demanded as Russell replaced Veta on her left.

He delivered the news in a flat monotone. "Prestamped and addressed from drop-off box downtown. No way to trace it. I'll have it checked for fingerprints just in case our friend was careless."

"He won't be."

Zach's silence said he didn't think so either. He didn't ask how she was doing, coming even more quickly to the point than Veta. It would have been nice to know he cared.

"In the future, you accept nothing yourself. Not packages, not phone calls, not visitors. Everything goes through me."

"Rule One."

"Exactly. Your employees have been advised of that, as well." A pause then right to the heart of it. "Tell me about the blouse."

Toni sucked a deep gulp of frigid air to help maintain her calm front. "I was wearing it when I was kidnapped."

His voice softened imperceptibly. "And the bloodstains on it?"

"Mine, I think." She closed her eyes, mentally flinching as she recalled the harsh slap in the van and the coppery taste that filled her mouth.

"I'll have it tested." He put up his hand to ward off her protest. "No worries. Strictly off the records and low key. A favor from a friend." Then his look grew more serious. "Who took it off you?"

"That's a dead end. Literally." She took another pull off the cigarette. The palsied tremor in her hand belied her cool summation.

"So, who would have kept it for ten years? And why? Where would it have been?"

"A souvenir? A trophy? I don't know." Frustration built in her tone as she considered the possibilities. "The other man was never caught. Maybe he was just biding his time until I came into money since he couldn't get any from my father the first time around." A patient premeditation. *Where's the money?* Her worst nightmare come true. "If only I knew what he wanted."

"You need to cancel tomorrow night's party."

Her reply was automatic. "No."

"So many people coming and going and in the house makes you more vulnerable."

She twisted in the chair to look up at him. He was staring out over the lake, his expression as inviting as those cold waters. "No. Hire more guards. Increase security. That's your job. My job is business as usual. I will not hide from this man. I will not give him the satisfaction of seeing me afraid."

But she was. And no matter how much bravado she flung up between them, he had to know it.

"We'll compromise. Throw your shindig tomorrow but no press conferences, no public appearances thereafter.

Low profile, just like you said. I can't cover all bases if you're the center of attention in a crowd."

Her acceptance was purely practical. "All right."

Zach squinted at her, doubting her sincerity. "No public PR things in Mexico, no opportunities for the bad guys to get close to you."

She shivered slightly. "Deal."

"In. Out. Back to business."

When she lifted the cigarette for another pull, Zach intercepted the movement, plucking the half smoked filter tip from her hand. He took one last long draw from it himself before flicking it away.

"Those are bad for you."

His bland pronouncement was the last straw for this already broken camel. "Bad for me? Having someone stalk and terrorize me is bad for me."

"But you can't control that. You can control what you choose to do to yourself. Like taking unnecessary risks with people who don't really matter."

"Thank you Dr. Freud. And I'll thank you to remember your own Rule Three. My personal habits are none of your concern, Russell, so back the hell off."

His level gaze never flickered. "They are if they make my job more difficult."

"Deal with it."

"My rules. My way."

Their stares battled for supremacy, then she finally relented with a stiff "Yes, sir."

He nodded. "Good girl. Now, what's on your plate for the rest of the day?"

With her thoughts and emotions so embroiled in the past, it was hard to focus on the hours of the day that remained. She took a deep breath to clear her mental slate. "About three hours worth of business calls. Nothing that you'd care to sit through."

"Your agenda is my agenda. Don't feel you have to entertain me."

"That was nowhere near the top of my list of concerns."

A faint smile crinkled the corners of his eyes. "You don't have to hurt my feelings."

Because she was thinking how seriously sexy that small smile made him, Toni's reply cracked with irritation. "As if that could happen."

His features settled back into their impassive lines.

Sighing with aggravation, she pushed up out of the chair. "Well, come on, then. Time to get back to work."

And work she did. Tirelessly. Aggressively. With a level of determination and energy that exhausted him as he watched and said nothing.

She had an office on the second floor that capped one end of the house. Three sides were glass. Instead of conventional heavy wood, the furniture was a light, airy wicker and the cushions splashed with bold colors. He stretched out on a surprisingly comfortable chaise while she made her calls to everyone from distributors, trucking companies and printers to talk show hosts, sport and fashion magazine editors discussing the move, the new spring merchandise and her succession to the throne of power. With her calendar and Rolodex flipping, she set up appointments in L.A., New York, and Dallas in the upcoming months and, true to her word, canceled those in Mexico. She treated each individual with charm, respect and an underlying authority. She was very good at her job.

Zach had to wonder why her father worried. The company was obviously in loving and capable hands.

Because the sight of her against the backdrop of the setting sun made a picture too achingly beautiful to behold for long, Zach closed his eyes, letting the crisp cadence of her voice become music to his weary soul. He stirred restlessly on the lounge, shifting to find a level of comfort that escaped him. His hand throbbed meanly. His eyes ached with the gritty burn of too little sleep but real slumber was a distant luxury he couldn't afford. Instead, he eased into the twilight state that served him while in the field when the ability to hear an enemy coming was the only thing that kept him alive. Dozing lightly on the edge of awareness, he considered the puzzle of his situation.

Why had Castillo requested his return? The man had done everything within his considerable power to have Zach dismissed from his position. Dereliction of duty and gross incompetence. The shame of it still burned like the sting of Jack's neat stitches. Ten years ago. He'd been so green. His first big assignment. And nearly his last. If it hadn't been for the respect his superiors had held for his father, he might have ended up selling those shoes the lovely Ms. Castillo manufactured.

And yet Castillo had sought out Jack, asking him to use his connections to find him in whatever hell hole he'd buried himself for the sake of Queen and country. He wasn't an easy man to find. He'd left above board intelligence work behind shortly after the fiasco with Antonia Castillo, sinking deeper and deeper into the covert mire until he was no longer sure which agency pulled the strings. But he never once wavered from his course. His were no longer the slick, debonair James Bond-type assignments, but he didn't mind getting his hands dirty for a good cause. As long as that cause allowed him a measure of justice. He was realistic enough to know that was all he would ever get.

Jack's offer of a job had taken him by surprise. Jack Chaney was one of the very few who understood Zach's true motives and knew they had nothing to do with the Royals or the Union Jack or duty or politics. It was something much closer, more personal than that. He touched the diamond stud he wore in his earlobe, twisting it the way he did when he needed a reminder of why he lived on a dangerous razor's edge for weeks, sometimes months, coming back to the only place he could vaguely call home to stay long enough to wash the grime and gore down the drain. Where he'd pretend for whatever hours that he could snatch away that he really was the urbane sophisticate his neighbors believed him to be. They'd never believe the truth. It was an illusion he protected zealously, a part of his heritage he couldn't surrender.

He'd agreed to Jack's request. The why was a complex issue. The easy answer, the one that would ride comfortably upon his conscience, was because Jack had asked him. There was precious little he wouldn't do in the name of their rare friendship. But it wasn't Jack. And it wasn't whatever Victor Castillo might think he was owed. It was for the girl with the shell-shocked eyes and victimized body who now wore the mask of normalcy as well as he did.

And for her, he would put aside his own agenda, if only for a little while, if only to give ease to that trauma he'd witnessed, but she'd had to survive.

It was hard to concentrate with him in the room.

Toni's glance touched upon his relaxed features. She

knew he wasn't sleeping. Behind the closed eyelids spun a busy mind, probably calculating the security avenues he'd have to take to put a lock down on the nightmare of tomorrow's party. All business, all the time. That was Zach Russell. Even then.

The next number she needed to call was on the card before her, but she wasn't looking at it. She was looking back.

She remembered the first time she'd seen him in the foyer below. He'd been young, mid-twenties, but already with such a foundation of control and potential. Polite, reserved yet capable of charming with a flash of that rare smile. He'd been so different from the other stoic automatons, she couldn't help being drawn to him. They were there to escort father and daughter to a business meeting in London. She didn't know what her father's business there entailed. She never asked. She'd grown up surrounded by his secrets and his security in one form or another so she didn't question the reasons why.

Glad for the distraction on what she considered a dreary trip, she insisted that the young and fiercely dedicated agent be assigned to her. She'd flirted with Russell mercilessly, determinedly, and though he retained a careful distance, he'd never made her feel foolish in her infatuation. He hadn't encouraged her, but she hadn't needed any. Despite what her father would later claim, he'd done nothing inappropriate. He just done…nothing. He hadn't provoked her dangerous response to his horribly proper rebuff. It wasn't his fault that he'd broken her heart, damn him and that stiff British civility.

"I'm done here."

Her announcement brought his eyes open and the coiled

readiness back into his partially recumbent form. He was on his feet by the time she came around the desk and they met at the foot of the lounger. Both pulled up short, startled by their sudden close proximity. And by the amazingly sharp recall of another moment so like this one, where awareness of one another took them by surprise and a blind-siding desire came close to overwhelming reason.

Neither moved as the unintentional happenstance built into a storm-charged intensity. Unguarded stares locked. As Toni gazed up into Zach's eyes, the mercurial green-gold flared with passionate possibilities. Possibilities she's once wanted to explore more than anything she could dream of. And perhaps, still wanted despite all that had happened between that first blush of innocent desire and now. All she had to do was reach out for the feel of his rock hard chest. All she had to do was stretch up for a sample of his unyielding lips. And in this brief instant with defenses down, he might have allowed it. He might have enjoyed it.

But he'd had his chance.

"Excuse me."

The intrusion of her rough-edged words brought sensibility snapping back into his cloudy stare. He took a quick step back and the moment was gone. Toni moved past him as if the encounter was already forgotten.

But all through dinner, at a table with a now distant Zach, her father and Veta and assorted business associates, her distracted thoughts quivered with tease of one what if.

What if she had kissed him ten years ago? How different, then, might her life have been.

Chapter 4

Her birthday. Her ascension to the top of Aletta. The house swarmed with the rich and powerful come to pay homage to both events. It was her night to shine, but Toni would have felt more comfortable had that light been under a basket. Because she was very aware that someone in the glittery crowd might have an agenda other than celebration, one that involved a blood-stained blouse and a ransom unpaid.

Her mother had trained her practically since birth to work a room, to make the most of her looks, her smile, her smarts. She did so on a gracious autopilot while her gaze scanned the shadowed corners and her system jumped at every unexpected sound. She searched for Zach, finding instead a host of unfamiliar faces he'd brought in for the occasion to police the room. The sight of those innocuous strangers brought no sense of comfort, though she was sure they were very good at their jobs. They had nothing at stake, no reason to go an extra mile, to make that extraordinary promise to secure her peace of mind. Only Zach Russell had done that.

Where was he?

She snagged a flute of champagne from a passing tray just to have something to do with her hands. She wouldn't drink. She needed her senses sharp.

Where the hell was he?

Every room of the house was designed for ease of entertainment and traffic flow. Each was crowded with guests intent upon sampling all they could from the elegant appetizers, abundant spirits and undercurrent of classical music served up to them with an unobtrusive style. She moved through the ground floor chatting with friends and business associates while her gaze never stopped its restless journeys and her nerves pulled ever tighter.

Even the stairs were lined with company who lifted their glasses in salute as she climbed past them. Her father was in the huge upstairs room that served as theater, boardroom and, as it did tonight, ballroom. The oriental rugs had been rolled back to expose the gleaming floor. An alcove at the far end hosted a five piece band playing an infectious ragtime. Through the bank of glass to the left was the dynamic view of the lake and to the right an equally impressive sea of imported luxury cars overflowing the drive and extra lot. And her father stood at the massive fireplace, leaning casually against the Danish tiles as he talked business. Even on this night, he was hard at work.

"Antonia, you know Servando Fuentes."

She took the cold, limp fingers offered by Angel Pre-

miero's right-hand man. Premiero, who'd grown up with
Victor Castillo, had partnered with her father in many of
his past ventures. Now he was spearheading the company
move to Mexico.

"Señor Fuentes, always a pleasure." She waited just
long enough to be polite before withdrawing her hand,
fighting the urge to scrub her palm to restore its warmth.

"Señor Premiero most anxiously awaits your visit and
the opportunity to link your families in business."

She smiled thinly. As long as that was all Premiero
thought to link. "I look forward to our meeting."

"Happy birthday. This is from Señor Premiero. A small
token."

Under the unbridled avarice of her father's stare, she
took the heavy velvet box and opened it with a hint more
apprehension than anticipation. Gifts from Premiero didn't
come unencumbered by strings.

It was a weighty necklace of silver fashioned into entwined calla lilies. The bell of each flower was filled with
a piece of deep blue lapis.

Fuentes waited with a smug smile for her reaction.
When it was slow to come, he prompted, "Señor Premiero
remembered those exquisite eyes you inherited from your
mother, may she rest with the saints."

"Put it on, Antonia," her father urged, but Toni was reluctant to wear Premiero's controlling collar quite this
soon. She shut the box and offered, instead, a pretty thank
you.

"Tell Señor Premiero his gift is as lovely as it is extravagant. I will wear it with something more appropriate
when we meet."

Her lack of enthusiasm over the gift clearly annoyed her

father, but she spotted Veta by the hall and took the opportunity to slip away with a nod and a wish for them to enjoy the evening.

Veta looked stunning in a full-length tank dress that skimmed her knockout figure with an explosion of grand scale red Impressionist roses upon a dark background. With her vivid makeup and black hair piled high, she looked like an exotic, hothouse species. But Toni knew she carried a .44 in her chic beaded bag. This rose had deadly thorns.

"Here." Toni thrust the box at her once they were in the hall. "Put this somewhere."

Veta opened the lid and expressed a low whistle. "Who's the admirer?"

"Premiero."

Veta closed the lid and regarded her friend solemnly. "Toni, how are you going to work with his man if you despise him so?"

"My father has worked with despicable characters all his life. It's part of doing business." That's what he'd always told her.

"But at what cost? Promise me you'll be careful. Premiero is no junior league executive to be easily controlled."

"As he thinks to control me with his gifts and his oily embassador? I know what Premiero is and what he's capable of."

"Do you?"

To lighten that dour warning, Toni placed her hand upon her friend's shoulder. "That's why I have you to run interference. One look at you in that dress and he'll be blinded by more than ambition."

Veta gave a derisive snort. "One uses what one has to its best advantage as your father would say."

"Yes, he would." Toni glanced about restlessly. "Have you seen Russell?"

"He asked me to stick close to you while he handled the perimeter. I guess he's not much of a social animal. Perhaps his tuxedo is at the cleaners."

That he would hand her off into the care of others rankled unexpectedly. Just as his intentional absence chilled her. "I'm not paying him to shake the bushes. He's supposed to be with me."

Veta raised a speculative brow, but offered no comment. "Last I saw him he was headed back toward the kitchen."

"I guess it's time I stirred something up with our Mr. Russell."

The kitchen, a gleaming bank of stainless steel and oiled butcher block, was a hive of activity with waiters rushing in and out, heat pulsing out from the big industrial oven and flames jetting from the multi-burnered stoves. Six cooks performed under the exacting maestro's baton of Henri Galliteau, a master chef stolen from one of the pricy Windy City restaurants her father favored. Henri conducted the chaos in his kitchen with a loud and often profane gusto, comparing the qualities of his underling chefs to the nether regions of a suckling pig while brandishing a cleaver as his instructional wand. No one was allowed in his kitchen during an event. Those performances were always closed to an audience. Which was why the sight of Zach Russell sampling a Bearnaise sauce at his side gave her a jolt of surprise.

He did own a tuxedo. And he looked fabulous in it.

"It's nice to know you'll have a skill to fall back on when this career is pulled out from under you."

Russell finished stirring the bubbling cheese mixture, then glanced up without a trace of surprise or chagrin. He'd known she was there. His gaze was cool in the sweltering kitchen.

"It's been tried before without success. A stellar reputation can survive a few dings and scratches."

"How about a head on collision?"

Henri murmured something to him in French and Zach smiled faintly, his gaze never leaving the challenge of Toni's.

He'd been ignoring her and now he was laughing at her. Her temper came to a hot, rolling boil.

"You're not being paid to entertain yourself playing Julia Child in my kitchen."

Unmoved by her harsh tone, Zach's reply was as nonchalant as his manner. "Not enjoying the party? Is that what's got your panties in a twist?"

All movement ceased in the room. Her fury escaped like steam from a pressure cooker, with a fierce hiss.

"Not so much as you, apparently. And, if my panties were a topic of discussion in front of the staff, be advised that I'm not wearing any."

As Toni stormed from the kitchen, every male eye was drawn to ascertain the truth of her parting statement, Zach's included, until the swinging door closed behind her.

"Excuse me, *monsieur,* I fear I've left something burning." Zach handed the ladle to Henri, who shook it at him with a knowing smirk.

"A few careful stirs will prevent scorching, *mon ami.*"

She stalked down the hall, heading for the escalating noise of the party. With a quick movement she bolted down the contents of the flute she still carried. It wasn't enough to extinguish her ire.

"You were in no danger." He spoke softly and suddenly from just over her shoulder.

"Not as much as you are at this moment." She refused to look at him.

"I thought you preferred head-on, but you seem to be enjoying these nasty sideswipes."

She stopped then to confront him directly. "What happened to your Rule Two? Or do you just impose them then break them at your discretion?"

He touched the almost invisible earpiece he was wearing. "I don't have to be right next to you to be right next to you."

"So you thought you'd play Iron Chef at my expense?"

Again, the slight quirk of a smile. "I was doing intel work."

"You think the kitchen staff is going to try to poison me?"

He grinned then, a quick startling flash of white. "The only thing venomous around here tonight seems to be your tongue." Then before she could parry that remark, he was all business once more. "Who notices the goings on in a big house better than those you never see?"

She took a breath. And another. He'd been working the staff for information. "Did you find out anything interesting?"

His gaze did a quick downward dip. "That you're not wearing any panties."

With a huff of aggravation, she spun away and marched back toward her celebration, which was now in raucous full swing. She didn't have to see Russell's grin. She could feel it.

Zach watched as she cut through the room like a social heat seeker. To appease her, he remained in plain sight just on the edge of the party while she controlled it.

The crowd loved her just as the camera loved her. How could they help it? She dazzled, with her beauty, with her rapier-sharp wit, with her flair for doing the unexpected.

In a sea of slinky evening gowns, she was the only woman who didn't feel the need to make a statement by showing lots of bare shoulders, cleavage and leg. Her heavy dark hair was pulled up severely into a knot at the crown of her head then hung in a thick braided tail. She wore an evening suit that revealed nothing yet still managed to be sexy and exotic. Her mandarin-style jacket covered her from neck to fingertips in black silk heavily embroidered and beaded with Oriental florals and banded at collar, cuffs and hem with swatches of stiff peridot brocade. Beneath the weighty jacket that extended just below her hips, she wore loose-fitting black trousers over flat black slippers.

And apparently no panties.

She was still angry with him. She let him know it with her occasional stabbing glances. He wasn't sure why he deserved it for just doing his job. But, having given up trying to decipher female logic—especially *this* female's logic—he accepted it and stayed out of range. To distract himself from the panty issue, he thought ahead, to the trip to Mexico, to the potential difficulties of protecting her in a foreign country while she dealt with a man whose questionable background paralleled her father's. Would she follow in their business footsteps, shunning integrity for a bigger bottom line? He wanted to think not. He didn't want to believe "like father, like daughter."

But she had let him take the fall to protect her father's reputation. He had never believed it was to save her own. For all her defiant bluster, Toni Castillo wanted to make her daddy proud.

Whether Victor Castillo was worth the effort or not.

As the hour grew later and the party wilder, Zach watched Toni loosen up as the number of drinks consumed overcame her concerns. She danced with the male guests, making each one of them from eighteen to eighty-five fall in love or lust with her. But while she'd do a sexy bump and grind, she refused to be drawn in close for the occasional slow song. What man wouldn't want to have her pressed into him for a languid, sensual sway? But she shook off their invitations with a laugh and a request for another champagne. Most took her evasion with a good-natured disappointment. But not all.

Jerry Middleton, son of the founder of Middleton Transport. Zach had done his homework on the guest list provided. A punk, a freeloader skating by on his father's money and depending upon his pull to keep him from doing serious time for any of his frequent tangles with law enforcement. Several of them included burying the complaints of former girlfriends who said Jerry liked to play rough.

And, apparently, Jerry didn't like to be told no. Especially in front of a crowd.

The first time he tried to push the issue, Toni simply walked out of his clumsy embrace and Veta stepped in to fill her place. Veta distracted him from his intentions and managed to whisper a warning for him not to cause a scene. The warning took, for all of fifteen minutes. Then he was back, cornering his hostess and trying to charm his way back into her good graces. Not wanting to offend him, Toni endured his attention but kept up the physical distance by placing her hand on his chest each time he tried to lean in closer.

He should have gotten the message, but some guys just needed a special delivery.

Jerry Middleton was becoming a rude bore.

Toni knew how to handle men. She did it with humor, with firmness and, if necessary, with force. But Jerry just wasn't getting it. He wasn't getting anything from her on this night or any other.

"Happy birthday, Antonia."

Toni turned gratefully toward one of her father's bankers and accepted a quick buss upon her cheek. But when he moved away and she looked back to confront her annoying pursuer, Jerry breeched her personal space with a husky, "I haven't given you a birthday kiss yet."

Alarm leapt inside her as he crushed her back against a credenza with the wall of his chest. Struggling to control the sudden acceleration of her heart and the instinctive surge of panic, she angled her head to present her cheek, but his hand forked beneath her chin, his fingers clamping tight. Fear, harsh and black, rose to choke her, wadding in her throat, suffocating the need to scream out in protest. Her brain shouted for her limbs to move, to shove him, to hit him, to knee him into submission, but her muscles locked into frozen acquiescence. And Jerry Middleton knew how to take swift advantage of a moment's weakness.

Her ability to think, to breathe was gone. As his features filled her field of vision, a familiar cold darkness seeped up to steal her sight away. A roar began in her ears, threatening to consume her until quiet words sliced through it with an edge of steel.

"Take a step back or I'll take you out like a sack of trash."

Middleton may have been drunk, but he wasn't stupid enough to miss the menace in that simple claim. He stepped back and found himself pinned by a dismembering stare.

"Mr. Middleton is ready to leave."

His arms taken on either side by two large uncompromising fellows, Jerry made his first smart choice of the evening. He didn't argue.

With the direct threat removed, Zach confronted the damage done. Toni looked through him with eyes blank and glassy. Her breaths came in shallow little gasps of fast approaching shock. There was no way to gracefully extricate her from the overcrowded room.

"Antonia, look at me." No response. "Toni, can you hear me? Nod if you hear me."

A short up-and-down jerk of her head. Good.

He pitched his voice low, the words soothingly smooth. "You wanted me to dance with you once upon a time. I think I'd like that dance now. What do you say? Will you dance with me, love?"

Very slowly he gathered her in his arms. She snapped rigid and for a moment he feared she would bolt. Her resistance held for several frantic beats and then she gave, just slightly at first but enough for him to ease her away from the wall and toward the offer of shelter in his embrace. When he felt the tentative touch of one hand at his waist, he lifted the other in his. Her fingers were deathly cold and still.

"That's it. You've never been afraid of me, Toni. Dance with me. I won't step on your toes."

He eased back and she followed. That was enough to encourage the loose circle of his other arm to tighten until she was leaning into him if not with complete trust, at least without objection. And he began to move with her, a slow, side to side shift, rocking her in the cradle of his arms. It was like dancing with a rag doll with only the stiff embroidery on her jacket to give her starch. He gave her time to recover, sheltering her from the curious by letting their revolutions carry them through the room and toward the full-length French doors leading out onto the empty patio.

Music filtered out after them only to be snatched away by a gust of wintery night air. He imagined the terrace with its smooth stone slabs edged by cement benches, where carefully trimmed hedges glistened with tiny twinkle lights, would be the popular spot for summer fetes but on this blustery night, they were quite alone. He guided her carefully away from the glare of the interior lights, past the central garden with its fountain and fauna stunted by the cold. He knew exactly when awareness returned to her, awakened by the brisk evening air. Her body jerked sharply. Her fingers spasmed, knotting in his coat, threading between his in a frantic twist.

"It's all right. You're safe with me."

Shaking her head slightly as if clearing it of sleep, she took an unsteady breath and let her tension go upon its exhalation. Then she collapsed against him, her head tucking beneath his chin, her arms burrowing inside his tux jacket to twine behind the satin back of his vest. And for a long moment she was content to remain like that, dependent upon his strength and his silent support. A rare lapse

into vulnerability that reminded him acutely of another
time when he held her this close to quiet her fears.

"Don't say anything. No one can know what happened."

"Have you ever seen anyone?"

"What?" Her toned was blurred by a poignant confusion that wrenched his gut as brutally as the old memory.
"Am I seeing someone? No."

"I mean professionally."

A pause. Then he felt her stiffen with understanding.

"You mean a shrink? No." That independent streak of
toughness hardened her reply, but she didn't relinquish her
hold on him. If anything, she tunneled in closer as if to distract him from this unpleasant thread of conversation.
"Why would I? I don't need to pay some head doctor to
tell me what my problem is."

"What's your problem, Antonia?"

He didn't think she was going to answer. He didn't
need her to tell him in words. He'd seen the stark truth in
her eyes inside, when terror overcame all logical responses
and shut down all her resources. She'd been one of the
walking wounded, shell-shocked, battered, broken and far
from healed. But the physical scars weren't the ones she
choose to address when she leaned back just far enough
to look up into his face. Hers was as pale as a piece of stat-
uary but her dark-centered gaze was hot in contrast to the
icy breeze. She recovered way too fast and was far too
good at covering up for any obvious transgressions.

"My problem, Russell, is guys who stick to the rules."

Her hands slid up the slippery sides of his vest, track-
ing its lapels until they reached the warmth of his neck.
Her fingertips brushed along the channel of his throat,
riding the sudden gallop of his pulse.

"I've wanted to do more than dance with you, Zach."

Temptation, hot and sweet, nearly drowned him in the long, languid moment it took for her to rise up ever so slowly on her toes, stretching up to take from the suddenly mindless slackening of his mouth. He felt the first exquisitely soft touch of her lips, breathed in the fragrant intoxication of her champagne-laced breath. And just as his eyes grew heavy lidded in surrender, reason served up a swift, ruthless slap.

He reared back, blinking away the blinding passion for what he knew was madness to desire.

He'd almost—

And she knew it.

And that made his last-ditch rejection all the more bitter for her pride to swallow.

"Thanks for the dance." Her voice sounded rusty but her stare was a whetted blade.

Before he could catch her, she spun out of his arms heading, not for the safety of the house, but for the unwelcoming darkness skirting the patio. She disappeared, leaving him to curse both his reaction and his lack of proper response that had hurt her yet again.

He hadn't brought a light and the blackness between the patio and the shimmer of the lake some 180 feet below was a complete unknown. He'd have to go after her. And while he searched that impenetrable darkness, he'd have to think of something to say that would ease the horrible awkwardness that passed for unrequited needs. He started to circle the stone rail, searching for an opening that would lead him after her.

And then he heard her cry out, one muffled sound too quickly muted.

Chapter 5

Stupid. Stupid. Stupid. Stupid.

The word exploded with each downward step she took into darkness.

Why was the only man who made her feel safe, the only one who could reach through the glassy pain of her past to stir feelings of normalcy, more intent on his duties than upon the desire she briefly ignited in his gaze? She'd made a fool of herself over him not once but now twice. You'd think she'd learn.

She paused on the narrow stone stairs that cross cut the steep bank, breathing hard into her humiliation. Awareness of her surroundings seeped in with a shiver. She should go back up to where Russell would be waiting to scold her for acting like an impetuous child. Where she'd have to meet his stare and see nothing but business in those cool, assessing eyes. Wasn't that what she wanted? Wasn't that the way she preferred it to be?

With every man but him.

Why was he the only one who found it so easy to resist her? Because she was just the job? Or because he thought she was spoiled and more than a little bit loopy? She sighed unhappily. Probably both. Around him, she felt that awkward, giddy eighteen all over again.

She remembered the way he'd looked at her on that drizzly London evening as she paraded in front of him in her blue spandex top and body hugging black leggings, coquettishly asking if he'd give her her first kiss as an adult. He'd been watching her with a tolerant amusement, but suddenly that look changed. Everything about him changed in some subtle, elemental way. His eyes had darkened to a smoky jade green that fascinated and shot a tiny electric thrill through her. And she'd taken a chance, looping her arms around his neck, reaching up for his mouth. His breath had been so warm and moist against her skin. And she'd wanted that kiss, wanted him more than anything before. Or since.

And then he'd come to his senses, just as he had this time. Denying her the chance to taste passion. The only memories she held now had nothing to do with pleasure, only pain.

Instead of returning to her party, she continued downward, needing the chill of the night to clear her head and a moment of isolation to gather her fragmented control. Having run these steps all her growing-up years, the darkness didn't hinder her progress. For once, she embraced it for the anonymity it provided. She'd been in the spotlight all her life, on display for everyone to see, to judge. For the moment, she just wanted to blend in to the background, unnoticed and unremarkable.

She reached the gravel service drive at the base of the hill. The sound of the waves created a soothing ambiance. Almost as calming as being rocked in Russell's arms. She shook off that memory with a soft curse and started to walk. Feeling the cold more intently, she banded her arms about herself in an insulating hug.

She heard the crunch on gravel behind her over the repetitive rush of the swells. Russell come to claim her, no doubt, come to tighten up the leash. She didn't slow her pace. Let him catch up. Being too much the proper gentleman, he'd never bring up her inappropriate behavior beyond chiding, *Rule Three, Ms. Castillo*. As if she was the flighty eighteen-year-old instead of the CEO of an international company. Well, he could take his Rule Three and—

She felt the movement rather than heard it, the sudden push of air behind her and suddenly next to her. Something whipped over her head and pulled taut about her throat, cold, cutting into tender flesh even as she managed a startled cry. Then the ability for sound was lost as a quick tightening about her neck shut off her airway. Blackness rose apace with terror. Over the roar in her head she heard a harsh warning whispered so close to her ear she could feel the heat of her assailant's breath.

"You aren't safe. He can't protect you. Only your money can save you. Prepare to pay."

"Toni!"

Zach!

Her world spun crazily as the pressure and pain at her neck was suddenly gone. She collapsed to hands and knees on the sharp pebbled drive, gasping for breath, struggling to form his name through the raw agony in her throat.

Bright, blinding light washed over her. She shielded her eyes with a shaky hand as silhouetted figures burst from the darkness to surround her. Hands, firm and strong, settled on her shoulders.

"Are you all right?" Brisk, efficient, all business and wonderfully familiar.

She managed a nod as she felt her neck and forced herself to breathe past the pain.

"Stay here."

While she knelt on the gravel in her own circle of illumination, lights slashed through the darkness like a laser show. She heard Veta's voice.

"What happened? Where's Toni?"

And then her friend was there to kneel beside her, to take her into a consoling embrace.

"Are you hurt? What were you doing down here alone? Where's Russell?"

Toni reacted to the anger in Veta's voice, instinctively trying to lessen Zach's part in her attack. "It was my fault." The words rasped out over the broken glass that seemed to line her throat. "I needed some air. I had too much champagne."

"So he just let you take a stroll down here by yourself? What was he thinking?"

"I was the one who wasn't thinking, Veta."

"Well, thank God you're all right. No thanks to your bodyguard who never seems to be where you need him."

Russell heard the recriminations as he approached and felt the truth of them cut harshly to his soul.

"Sir, I found this."

Zach shone his borrowed flashlight's beam on the item held out to him. It was a scrap of fabric. "Where?"

"In the briars over there. It looks like our assailant cut through the brush when he heard us coming. Must have cut himself up pretty good."

Zach study the swatch of black fabric and, indeed, found traces of blood on the ragged edges.

"Be careful with it. It's the only fingerprint we've got to point us in the right direction."

The swirl of lights converged where he was standing. The final report was unwelcome, but what he'd expected.

"No sign of him, sir."

"Party's over. Check the guests discreetly as they leave to see if any of them are missing part of their attire."

"Shouldn't we call the police?"

He glanced at the huddled figure, hearing her frightened voice in his head and allowing it to direct his actions now, as it had then. "And have them mucking about? We've got a plane to catch tomorrow and no time for their questions. I want a patterned sweep through here at first light to see if we can come up with anything else."

Only then did he turn his full attention to where Toni and Veta were getting to their feet. Toni was trembling with cold and delayed shock while Veta was cloaked in a hastily snatched man's overcoat. Zach slipped out of his jacket and draped it about Toni's quivering shoulders. Using his light, he studied her neck, seeing the beginnings of bruising and odd abrasions. Before he could ask, she held up a heavy necklace made of sterling. It had been used to choke her, its irregular design causing the lacerations in her skin.

"A birthday gift from Angel Premiero," she explained. "Callas. How almost prophetic."

"I gave the box to Muriel to put in your room," Veta was saying. "With all the guests roaming around, I don't know if we'll be able to narrow down who might have gone in to take it."

"Antonia?"

Victor Castillo burst into the gathering like a battering ram. His gaze took in his daughter's pale features and the circling marks about her throat, then he turned furiously to Russell for an answer.

"How did this happen?"

"My fault," Zach admitted stiffly. "A lapse in security."

"A lapse in judgment bringing you into this apparently," he bellowed. "My daughter could have been killed."

Toni placed a hand upon his sleeve. "That wasn't his intention," she stated quietly. "It was a warning. No harm done."

Her father examined her neck more closely. "That's not how it looks to me. I suppose makeup can cover those marks. No official report was called in, was it?" He glared back at Russell, concern rapidly shifting from his daughter's well-being.

"No, Father," Toni answered for him, her tone flat and final. "We'll keep it in house. No sense in stirring up publicity." She gathered Zach's jacket more closely about herself and started back for the stairs, leaving her father to grill Veta and the others about the lack of professionalism. She flinched slightly as Zach's hand cupped her elbow. They began to climb together, following the pool of light he shone ahead. They'd reached the first landing before he spoke.

"About what happened," he began.

She cut off his awkward apology with a wave of her hand. "Nothing happened. Nothing's going to happen. You were right, Russell. It's all about following the rules. I won't make that mistake again."

* * *

After the always arduous preparation for international flight and the exhausting crush in the airport, the plane lifted off as scheduled with Toni's party commandeering all of first class. Advertising and marketing hunched with sunglasses on and window shades pulled down, suffering the effects of too much party while the camera and make up people argued incessantly about the latest fashion trends and diet gurus. Usually, Toni liked to sit in the first row of seats with all the hubbub happening behind her so she could work on her lap top or dictate memos. But Russell insisted they take to row against the divider between the classes. So no one could come up behind them, she supposed. Zach plopped her in the window seat while he went to scope out the passengers and flight personnel. From her seat across the aisle, Veta, who hated to go any higher in the air than the top of three inch heels, was signaling for a preflight cocktail. She'd have a battalion of little bottles lined up before they landed.

She took a long swallow, sighed, then turned to Toni.

"Mateo called this morning. He can't wait to see you."

"You mean us."

"I'm his sister. You're his best friend. And if I'm not mistaken, he'd like the chance to change that."

Pretending not to understand the insinuation because it sparked a slight jump of unexpected alarm, Toni cried in mock dismay, "He doesn't want to be my friend anymore?"

Veta snorted. "I told him he was wasting his time, that you'd never take him seriously."

"When is Mateo ever serious about anything?"

"You might be surprised. Running the resort has matured him."

"You mean running after all the wealthy ladies staying at the resort has exhausted him."

"All I'm saying is look closely at the man he's become. He's been working very hard to be considered a success in your eyes."

That surprised Toni. They'd grown up together, the three of them as close as true family. "Mateo doesn't have to impress me."

"Every man thinks he has to impress you," Veta corrected, then glanced up as Russell returned from economy class. "Except that one."

Mood soured by that truth, Toni sat up straighter in her seat and pretended to be interested in the final boarding preparations going on outside the window as her bodyguard took the aisle seat beside her. She both hated and craved the sense of security that came with him situating himself between her and the rest of the world.

"Everything all right?" She tried to make her tone nonchalant even as her hand went self-consciously to the bright designer scarf loosely knotted at her throat.

"Fine. Buckle up."

As she bent to retrieve her errant lap belt, the thin leather portfolio resting on her knees slid to the floor. Both of them leaned down at the same time placing their faces in an unexpectedly close proximity. Her gaze flashed up only to be lost in the briefly unguarded intensity of his. Against the charcoal-colored wool of his coat, his eyes were as slated as the winter sky. But not cold. The heat she discovered there seared to the soul.

Too quickly he straightened, letting her snatch the

folder from his hand. As she returned to her proper upright seated position to prepare for take off, he said, "She's wrong."

"Who?"

"You've always impressed me."

With that claim, he shut his eyes and maddeningly proceeded to sleep, unmoving, until the pilot announced their descent into Mexico.

Toni tried to work.

In their fifth hour of the trip, crossing their third time zone, the passengers had settled into a quiet restlessness, watching a comedy movie on the small overhead screens or sleeping in awkward huddles. Too wired to do either, Toni studied the spreadsheets on her tray table.

Was she doing the right thing? Was this what her mother would have wanted for the company?

Her father and all his financial experts assured her that the move was the only way to save Aletta. They never seemed to see the faces of those who'd toiled their whole lives on the lines, on the docks, in the trucks, to bring their product to the consumer. Faces etched with betrayal and fear of an uncertain tomorrow. Emotions she understood. Not their responsibility, her father had said. Was that true? Perhaps, but it didn't make it feel right.

Had those workers, those loyal employees been angry enough to scare and attack her?

She didn't pursue the question. She put it away, packing it down tight with all the other unpleasantries she'd suffered just as her father had taught her. Don't react. Just go on. Rise above those things that frighten you.

She touched the ring she wore on her pinky finger. The

three twists of precious metal represented the past, the present and the future, her mother had told her. All entwined, all connected, not independent of the other. What would her mother have wanted her to do?

It was late and she was too tired to think clearly. She glanced beside her, quickly realizing her mistake when she couldn't look away from the chiseled strength of Zach's profile. After he'd returned her to her room the previous night, she'd taken one of her pills to find a saving rest but she suspected he'd spent the entire night awake and on alert. Watching over her.

Her protector. Her rescuer. If only he could save her from her greatest fear, not of putting herself out in the public eye where she'd once again be a target for anyone who thought to take advantage of her celebrity and fortune, but that when the popularity waned and she had all the money she could ever desire, that she'd spend the rest of her life alone without ever knowing the touch of love.

With a sigh, she reached up to switch off the overhead light, plunging their small area into darkness. After shifting uncomfortably for several minutes, she relented and gave in to her innermost need to reach out for a companionable warmth.

Zach Russell's shoulders were broad enough to carry the world, but on the last leg of their flight they had to support only one weary head.

The airport at Zihuatanejo was a square of blacktop surrounded by palm trees. No gate was pushed up to the door to ease their walk into the terminal in air conditioned comfort. The doors opened and weary passengers were met with the full brunt of humidity and a set of steps leading down to the tarmac. No smoothly efficient turntable carried luggage around for inspection. Bags were dragged out and left for lethargic travelers to find and muscle into the terminal. Then the long line to clear customs surrounded by cranky children, short tempered parents and the inevitable complainers while overhead ceiling fans stirred air so thick it was almost impossible to breathe.

Welcome to Mexico.

The parking lot was crowded with tour buses hosted by smiling natives in loud tropical shirts. Veta, who now had her land legs, herded their exhausted group toward a large hotel van with the name Royale Pacifico emblazoned on the side. As Zach started toward it, struggling under the bulk of Toni's bags, a familiar voice intruded.

"Let me get those for you, Mr. Russell."

Tomas, the Castillos driver, was quick to relieve him of the majority of the luggage, tossing it efficiently into the back of a compact rental car. When he held open the rear door, Toni crawled in without a word and Zach followed. They were out of the chaotic lot and on the road in mere minutes.

"You're a lifesaver, Tomas," Toni murmured as she burrowed into the seat with eyes closed.

"Your father pays me well to be, Miss Castillo. I flew down yesterday to make all the transportation arrangements."

"Know your way around, do you, Tomas?"

The young man's gaze met Zach's in the rearview. "I grew up in Zihua. My family still lives there. If there's anything you need, come see me. I can get you the best price for Cuban cigars, for silver, for…entertainment. You name it, Tomas can find it for you."

Zach smiled at the driver's enthusiasm. "You're a handy fellow to know."

"*Sí*, Mr. Russell."

"We'll talk."

Tomas held Zach's penetrating stare for a long silent moment then nodded. He passed a simple business card over the seat. "My pager number is on there."

Pocketing the card, Zach leaned back into the stiff seat. Quite the little entrepreneur. Perhaps one who could help him obtain certain items customs refused to let slide through. Toni appeared to be dozing so he turned his attention to what he could see of the countryside. Beyond the well-maintained highway bordered by rock walls and high fences, there was little to see but darkness until Tomas slowed. Ahead were guard shacks on either side of the road and outside them stood men armed with automatic weapons. Tomas showed his ID and they motioned him on with the tip of an assault rifle. They crested a hill and beyond was a valley of lights leading to the ocean.

"Ixtapa," Tomas announced.

"It seems well protected."

"A lot of tourist money is down there. We don't want any unpleasantness to scare them away."

"Is that the reason for the fences?"

"There's a jungle on the other side and a world our fancy visitors don't want to see."

"I've seen it."

Tomas glanced in the mirror. "I believe you. It's my job to see that Miss Castillo and her group stay on this side of the fence."

"That's my job, too."

Tomas nodded. "Not always an easy job."

"No, not always."

"If I can help, page me."

Zach patted his pocket.

Ixtapa was a resort haven, its boulevard lined with massive hotels on the ocean side and local tourist traps on the other. The Royale Pacifico sat back from the street behind white brick walls, its eleven-story tower gleaming against the near midnight sky. Tomas maneuvered them up the cobbled circle drive to the open air entrance to the lobby. When the car stopped, Toni stirred and came to life. She leaned across Zach's lap to scan the scattering of uniformed staff awaiting the new arrivals. As Tomas opened the door, she gave a squeal of delight and scrambled with a distressing agility over Zach's knees to exit before him. And raced right into the waiting arms of another man.

Observing Zach's tight expression, Tomas offered, "I'll see to the luggage, Mr. Russell."

"Right."

Zach approached the exuberantly hugging couple. When she noticed his stoic presence, Toni regarded him with a grin, still very much in the Ricky Martin lookalike's embrace.

"Russell, this is my oldest, dearest friend, Mateo Chavez, Veta's baby brother."

"Not a baby, Antonia, if you hadn't noticed," the handsome young man scolded. If Toni didn't, Zach certainly did as Chavez managed to detach one arm long enough to offer his hand. "Mr. Russell, the Royale welcomes you."

"Mateo owns the Royale," Toni explained proudly. "That's the reason we picked Ixtapa for our meetings rather than Mexico City."

"Ahh, you only came because of a friends and family

discount." The wounded tone was belied by an ear-to-ear flash of charm.

Antonia slapped his tuxedoed chest. "You know that's not true. Tomorrow you can show me everything but right now I need a room and at least twelve hours of sleep."

"Right away." He produced a key. "You are in the junior suite on eleven. I would have put you in our master suite, but Señor Premiero insisted it be held for his arrival."

"He's not here yet?"

"He was delayed by some business in Puerto Vallarta. Don't worry. I will keep you entertained until he arrives. The sun, sand and Royale are at your disposal."

"Oh, Mateo, you are a love." She stretched up to press a kiss to his smooth cheek and for a moment the grin faltered.

Something unpleasantly akin to jealousy gripped Zach's gut as he recognized the look Mateo Chavez gave her. There was nothing brotherly about it. Then his features brightened.

"There's my sister. I'll let Pablo take you to your room while I see the rest of your friends settled. And Mr. Russell will be staying where?"

"With me."

If Mateo drew any conclusions from her brief reply, he didn't display them. He held up the key and a sleek staff member took it from his hand. "Pablo, see our guests to their room."

As Mateo Chavez stood in the rapidly filling lobby watching the glass elevator carry Toni and her companion up through the open atrium, he felt his sister's hand upon his arm.

"Who is that man and what is he to Antonia?"

"He's no problem to our plans, *hermano*," Veta assured him as she followed his petulant glare. "You concentrate on wooing Toni and I'll see to Mr. Russell."

Chapter 6

Toni wasn't sure what woke her. She thought it was thunder, but when she slit her eyes open to look out the sliding doors, a cloudless blue sky greeted her.

She stretched languidly in the king-size bed and glanced at the digital clock on the night stand. Nine o'clock, she realized in some surprise. She hadn't slept in past 5:30 since high school and her sudden slothfulness was out of character.

Drawn by that blue sky after months of dismal Chicago winter, she rolled out from under the covers and went to pull back the patio slider. The rumbling sound intensified and she realized what it was. It was the surf rolling in on the endless miles of golden beach below. Warm air settled against her skin like a lover's caress as she took in the surroundings. The large hotel pool, which was separated from the ocean by a strip of sand and parade of thatched palapa

umbrellas, was already ringed by sunseekers in white
lounges and the chaises not yet taken were claimed by towels and summer read novels. A few colorful blow up rafts
dotted the inviting water and a group of children sluiced
down the twists of two waterslides.

Heaven.

"The shower's all yours."

Russell's voice startled her from her idyllic musings.
She'd forgotten he was there. The pull out couch was al-
ready made up and his travel belongings stored away.
Only her suitcases sat piled outside the spacious closet.

The sight of Zach Russell emerging from the bathroom
wearing a pair of snug jeans sapped the breath from Toni's
lungs. What usually was hidden beneath tailored suits was
a body cut with ruthless perfection. Shoulders and arms
swelled powerfully. Hard pectorals rode six-pack abs defined beyond a bodybuilder's wildest dream. She worked
out religiously but had never seen his sculpted equal in any
gym.

Wow.

Oblivious to her detailing stare, he crossed to the desk
chair to retrieve a white polo shirt. The muscles in his back
performed marvelous acrobatics as he slipped it over his
head. Before he could turn and catch her tongue hanging
out, Toni raced into the bathroom.

The room smelled deliriously of shaving soap and wet
man. His kit had been tucked away and damp towels neatly
folded. A pair of grey gym shorts hung on the back of the
door. The ambiance was intimately, excitingly male. And
to Toni, totally foreign.

She cranked on the water. To cold.

When she emerged from the bathroom wrapped in a

Royale robe, Toni was brutally awake and testily aware of the difficulties of sharing living space with her bodyguard. It wasn't crowded space. The suite was large, formed in a slight V with her massive bed and dresser in one portion. A central table and chairs, wet bar, desk and television made a visual divider leading to the social area with sleeper sofa, comfortable barrel shaped chairs, coffee table and second TV. Either section had it own awesome view and patio with glass-topped table and two plastic chairs. Zach stood out on the patio on his side, a cup of coffee in hand. He didn't turn, affording her some privacy as she tossed her baggage on the bed and nervously rooted through for clothes to wear. Rule Two took on a new meaning. Zach Russell with her morning, noon, night…all night. To think she'd joked about having him scrub her back.

She paused in what might have passed for virginal panic.

But then, why was she worried? Being the consummate professional, Russell would never breach her private space. For right now, considering all she had on her mind, that provided a measure of comfort. Business and personal emotions didn't mix. Her mother had taught her that and her father proved it by example. Their marriage had been one of appearance and cool civility, placing the bottom line before private time, of which there never seemed to be any. She learned by watching them negotiate their marriage the way most did a corporate merger. If passion played a role in it, that part had run its course long before she was born. If they'd sought to kindle fires outside of wedlock, they'd done so discreetly and without her ever knowing about it. Appearance was everything. A personal life was no dif-

ferent from the product they sold—it had to be of supe-
rior quality and without any defects. Perhaps Victor and
Mercedes Castillo had been able to maintain that facade
without difficulty. Toni found it a daily struggle. And part
of the reason was sharing her room.

She slipped into baggy gauze harem pants and a form-
hugging cropped tank top, then once a light application
of makeup was in place, Toni felt ready to confront her
roommate.

She heard his voice when she reentered the room and
continued toward him because she thought he was speaking to her. By the time she saw the cell phone at his ear,
she was too close not to overhear his conversation.

"I'm sorry I ruined your plans for the holidays. I meant
to share them with you."

Swallowing her surprise was like choking down her
own foot.

"Probably a couple weeks," he continued, not yet aware
of her presence. "I'll stop by then. I want to. I don't like
you spending so much time alone. Besides, I need to give
you your gift." He laughed and the sound seemed achingly
personal. "No, not prettier, just different. And just a job,
so you needn't draw any conclusions." His voice lowered,
becoming a rumble of affection that tore through Toni's
heart. "Miss you. I love you, too. I will. Jack told you? No,
no more stitches. I promise." He glanced over his shoulder then to catch Toni frozen by guilt. He closed the phone.
"I wasn't sure I could catch a relay down here."

"I'm sorry. I didn't mean to eavesdrop," she stammered.

Zach shrugged as if it was of no consequence that she'd
witnessed the tender exchange. "I'm ready for breakfast.
How about you?"

She nodded stiffly, wondering how she was going to coax an appetite past the knot in her belly.

Rule Three apparently didn't apply beyond the two of them.

While Toni sat at the bold Callas tiled table in the airy café nibbling on her plate of fresh fruit and sipping papaya juice and strong dark coffee, she watched in some bemusement as Zach had their good-natured server explain in detail every dish on the buffet bar down to ingredients and where they were grown. Then he had the rotund griddle cook giggling like a school girl as he chatted with her in perfect Spanish and flirted while she created his made-to-order omelet which he topped with fresh pico de gallo and fried black beans. Toni eyed his heaping plate when he finally joined her.

"There's not a single thing on there that's healthy, you know."

He paid her jaundiced comment no mind but instead forked off a morsel from the corner of his dish. "Try this."

"No, thank you."

"The texture of this flan is amazing. And this sauce. It's kiwi. Taste."

"No, I really don't—"

But he had the fork heading for her face and it was open or have it up her nose.

"What do you think? Sinful, isn't it?"

Though she agreed, she told him, "I think you have a curious fixation with food. Are you seeing someone for that?"

He grinned and her heart gave an anxious jump within her chest. It settled down only when his attention returned to his mammoth breakfast.

"I studied to be a sous chef once upon a time in my wastrel youth. I found the chemistry of mixing flavors fascinating."

"But you settled for mixing plastique, instead."

He went still for a moment then said nonchalantly, "Life has a way of changing your priorities."

She would have pursued the intriguing tidbit of information if Mateo hadn't picked that time to join them.

"*¡Hola!*" The handsome resort owner bent to press a kiss to Toni's cheek. "Enjoying your stay so far?"

"Looking forward to the pool and some sun," Toni confessed. "I haven't had a lazy day for far too long. What do you recommend?"

"Water volleyball, margaritas at the swim-up bar, a massage and sauna before siesta then a nice nap to get ready for the Mexican Fiesta tonight."

"I think I've just hired you to become my personal secretary."

"I'll leave that to Veta. She's much more capable." Mateo pulled up a chair, only then glancing at an expressionless Russell. His focus went right back to Toni. "My sister tells me you have had some trouble. We can't have worry putting lines on such a pretty face."

"A few lines add character," Zach interrupted smoothly. "But thanks for your concern." At Mateo's slight frown, he continued with a brisk authority. "I'll want to meet with your head of hotel security this morning. Also, I noticed some heavily armed fellows in flak jackets coming off the beach this morning."

"Our local police. They patrol the area to keep our guests safe."

"Is there a problem?" Toni's voice edged with alarm.

"I forget that though this is your father's home, you're not as familiar with Mexico. This is passionate country, a poor country, not so civilized as your United States. Rebellion is always boiling just under the surface. Our criminals are very bold. Every effort is made to insure our guests' safety, but you mustn't leave the resort area or venture off into the hills alone. Some of these rogues make a very good living by purse snatching and kidnapping. Not a fact we're proud of, but one we can't hide."

"She'll be protected."

Zach's flat summation drew a nod from Mateo. "That is good to know. My people will cooperate fully. Just tell them what you need. Antonia's safety is my primary concern." Then the charm was back as he snatched up her hand. "And so is your entertainment. Finish your breakfast and put on your swimsuit. I will take the day off so we can play as we did as children."

Zach was about to interrupt when he saw the expression on Toni's face. The angles softened with happiness and anticipation. Did he have the right to take that from her, to force her into the role of anxious victim once again?

"Come," Mateo urged with an engaging grin. "Let's sign you up for a massage. We offer eighteen different methods and all are guaranteed to melt you into butter."

Toni started to rise, then checked her enthusiasm with a look to Zach. The guarded disappointment settling over her features was enough to have him think, *what the hell.*

"I won't be far if you need me."

Toni's smile warmed like a sunrise.

"She won't," Mateo assured him with a bit of smug male posturing as he banded her tiny waist with the claim of one arm. As he led her away, Zach was already regretting the latitude he'd given.

"She'll be safe with him."

Zach stood as Veta joined him at the table. As vibrant as one of the tropical flowers in a boldly printed sarong and matching bikini top, sensuality wafted from her like a powerful fragrance. And she was well aware of the effect. She picked a piece of fruit from Toni's plate and sucked at it leisurely. A gesture Zach was sure was designed to distract a man from his higher cerebral functions.

"Convince me," he challenged mildly. "Tell me about your brother and their history."

"My mother was Victor's distant cousin. When she wanted to get us out of Mexico and into the States, she appealed to him to give my father a job. He worked down here as a policeman and she feared for his safety and our future. Victor brought us into his home and welcomed us like family. He made my father his head of security. My mother opened her own shop doing tailoring and alterations for all the Lake Shore debutantes. Mateo and I were raised like brother and sister with Antonia from the time we started school."

"And how did you get along?"

"Mateo and Antonia were wild and impetuous children. I was older and kept them out of trouble. I still do and I take that responsibility very seriously. I have been friend, sister and mother to Antonia since our mothers died in the same car accident."

Empathy for the tender-aged Toni fisted about his heart. "How old were you?"

"Toni and Mateo were fourteen and I was seventeen. It was very hard on them and on my father. He began drinking to escape the pain and loneliness. He was on a week-long drunk at the time Toni was kidnapped. He never got over it and retired right after she was returned to us. I took over his responsibilities then. It seemed only right." Veta told the story with an off-handed candor as if she were far distanced from the upheaval in her own young life. It got Zach wondering if that were true.

"So you lost your chance for freedom to babysit a spoiled heiress."

That got the sharp reaction he intended. Veta's dark eyes narrowed fiercely and her tone thinned to a razor's edge. "I lost nothing, Mr. Russell. I gained a position I enjoy and the satisfaction of helping a very capable and worthy woman whom I adore achieve a success she deserves. Toni's had nothing handed to her. She's earned everything she's gotten. If you think otherwise, you don't know her at all."

"I don't have to know her to protect her."

"There's where you're wrong, Russell. If you'd taken the time to know her, she would never have been taken from us. Don't make that same mistake again or I will make you very sorry."

She pushed away from the table without giving Zach a chance to rebut her accusation.

In truth, there was nothing he could say to disclaim her brutal words. She'd pinned the guilt straight to his soul and there was no way to wriggle free of it.

So he went about his business that morning, meeting with hotel security, briefing them on the situation and potential risks involving Toni's presence in the resort. He found them to be somber professionals who could be trusted.

As he sat that afternoon in the café, his presence carefully shadowed and obscured, he watched Toni frolic with her childhood friend as if she had no cares. While she played water volleyball at the whistle punctuated direction of the resort's activities director, Javier, who shouted encouragement in both English and Spanish over the loud pumping beat of American club mixes, Zach was mentally cataloging who might have the most to gain if Toni faltered and failed as CEO of Aletta. The more he considered the wronged union members, the least likely they seemed to play out as chief villain. The earlier threats and the recent events implied an intimate knowledge of Toni's past and that narrowed the scope of possibilities. But if that knowledge was for sale, virtually anyone could have orchestrated the escalating intimidation. Would those threats follow her here? He had to assume so. It was his job to presume so.

While she basked in the sun sipping Mexican beer, he was placing relayed calls to Jack Chaney requesting an investigation into Mateo Chavez's resort and the deaths of Mercedes Castillo and Mateo's mother.

And when Antonia emerged from the pool, flinging the wet sheet of her hair back, her strong body glistening as water beaded up on well-oiled skin, he tore his gaze from the spectacular sight to make a page.

"Tomas, Russell. I need some hardware and special equipment. How good are your connections? Can you hook me up?"

Veta was wrong about one thing. He did know Toni, perhaps better than anyone else. And there was no way he was going to fail her a second time around.

Chapter 7

It almost felt as if the last ten years had fallen away, leaving her soul delightfully carefree and spirit unscarred.

Even knowing the illusion wouldn't last, that the responsibilities and worries were still there waiting, Toni indulged in the escape the momentary break afforded. She could pretend Mateo was, again, her playful companion and that she had no concerns other than what to wear for the evening's fiesta. Her competitive nature slipped into overdrive during an exhausting two rounds of volleyball. A wonderfully mind-sapping soak in the sun was followed by the cool shock of pool water upon lotion-basted skin. Relaxation that had been so absent in her life was an intoxicating tonic she wanted to drink in for the rest of her stay.

She hadn't seen Russell all day. Knowing he was there somewhere gave her the sense of security to unwind without his visual reminder of what possible threats might still be close at hand. She didn't want to think about danger and the demons that relentlessly pursued her. She wanted to have fun, to cut loose, to be just another tourist at least until Premiero arrived to call her back to work. She deserved the R&R and Russell's grim rules weren't going to ruin it for her.

He wasn't in the room when she went up to change for the fiesta but his essence was everywhere. His clothing hung neatly beside hers. His aftershave lingered in the towels. She got looking at those skimpy athletic shorts and the desire to see him in them caused a brief short circuit to her motor skills. By the time she was dressed, she was agitated beyond reason without knowing why. Or not wanting to admit that she did.

The peppy sound of traditional music greeted her when the elevators opened in the lobby. And so did Zach. Dressed in casual khakis and a white linen shirt, he looked cool, relaxed and annoyingly appealing when he cocked his elbow toward her. She slipped her hand through that warm bend and allowed him to lead her out to the festivities.

The grassy area on the side of the hotel was ringed with twinkling lights and booths hawking local wares. The greeters slipped an earthen cup on a ribbon over their heads and filled it with a shot of tequila. With the bite of native liquor heating from the inside the way the damp hug of humidity did from the outside, they were guided in to a maze of tables where other resort guests were already clustered. They were placed at a large table with several other couples and a pair of college coeds on spring break. After sketchy introductions were made over the boisterous music, one of the men in a loud tropical print shirt, proudly proclaiming that he'd won the trip by being top salesman for his territory in Minnesota, bought them all a round of margaritas and told their server to keep them coming.

"So you all are from Chicago," one of the ladies leaned close to shout. She was probably in her fifties, dressed as if she was twenty and fried to a painful crimson. "You look like newlyweds."

Zach covered Toni's hand with his own. "That's right. I'm a day trader and my lovely wife teaches third grade."

Toni arched a brow at him and jumped in to redirect the conversation. "That's a beautiful necklace."

"I practically stole it down at the market in Zihua. Flash American dollars and you can talk these people into almost giving their silver away. I'd feel guilty if I wasn't getting such a fabulous deal."

The loud salesman who must have been the woman's husband took that moment to vent, "They deserve it. These people don't have the same value of money and standard of living that we do. They're stealing our American jobs and doing them for pesos on the dollar, putting hardworking U.S. families on welfare. Those fat cats at the head of our industries just wave a greenback and they scramble to snatch up our livelihoods. It's a crime is what it is. Hey, Pancho, bring another rum punch for my wife, poor favor."

The server who'd been standing behind him during the diatribe smiled and nodded, but his eyes glittered resentfully. Obviously he knew more English than the obnoxious drunk gave him credit for. Toni pressed her lips together tightly to refrain from comment, though she longed to remind the man that he was a guest in this country and should mind his manners. A quieter inner voice was asking if his sentiments were the same ones eating away like toxins at the workers in her own factory. Perhaps poisoning them to the point of striking out at her in their frustration?

The silver-draped woman laughed and shared with a pseudo-charitable attitude, "My Manny gave some ragged little Mexican boy a dollar to carry our bottled water from the store across the street. You would have thought we were feeding his family for a week."

"You probably were," Zach murmured agreeably. When the perpetually smiling server returned, Zach spoke to him in a Spanish aside and slipped him some coins. Toni heard the phrase Ugly American and the tone of apology, and felt vindicated for her country's rudeness.

Thankful to escape the offensive salesman, Toni followed the crowd to the buffet tables with Zach close behind her. While she juggled two plates, he did the loading to keep his hands free. She could see his interest in the platters of native dishes but he kept his inquiries on an olfactory level because of the crush behind them. As they were headed glumly back to their table, Bryce Tavish, her photographer, intercepted them.

"We can fit two more at our table. Join us. I need to go over tomorrow's shoot with you before I'm too drunk to speak intelligibly."

That's all the convincing it took to elbow in to the group that included Tavish, his pretty assistant Teddy, and two of the stylists who'd found themselves hunky beach boy dates. As he promised, Bryce jumped right into business first, outlining his plans for the advertising theme that would tie Aletta to its new location south of the border.

They would feature Toni pursuing various action-oriented activities from a mild bout of beach volleyball to parasailing and wave runners. She watched Zach's features harden into stone as he considered the security nightmare ahead.

"And for the grand finale," Bryce gushed with a flamboyant enthusiasm, "picture you rappelling up a mountainside then ziplining to the jungle floor. Baby, our marketing department will go absolutely gaga."

Zach made a gagging sound beside her. "Isn't that a little dangerous just to sell shoes?"

"Darling, Aletta isn't about shoes," Bryce explained patiently. "It's about attitude and mental toughness. And our Toni has it all. That's what the consumer wants. They want to be her. They want to be taking those risks, living that life on the edge."

"So she goes out on that edge to give them a vicarious thrill."

"You got it. That's what it's all about. That sweet faced Mateo is setting everything up for us. Don't frown like that. Wrinkles age the skin prematurely."

What was aging Zach was the situation being pulled farther and farther out of his control. He liked things in close and buttoned down tight where the exposure was limited and the advantage was theirs. Putting Toni out into wide open spaces or into activities that were inherently risky made his job more difficult. The more players on the scene, the higher chance of something going wrong. If he had his way, Toni would be locked in the hotel suite until the individual or group who was threatening her was locked away for good.

But one glance at her, at the mulish set of her chin and

the defiant flash of her eyes, and he knew that plan was doomed to failure.

"I'll have to chat with sweet-faced Mateo," he grumbled.

Toni pressed his arm. The contact was brief and impulsive. It caught him off guard as did the sudden shock of heat that shot straight to his belly like an unexpected bite into a jalapeño. He was saved from further distress by the start of the night's entertainment.

The fiesta presented Mexican history in a colorful and dramatic pageant of song and ceremony, from the fierce heart-pounding drumbeats leading caped and feathered warriors through the ritual of human sacrifice to sombrero-topped mariachis. And as the heavy heat of the evening settled along with the effects of the margaritas and rum punches, Toni swayed to the peppery rhythms, a smile on her face and her eyes half closed. Zach's nose was full of her lime-and-coconut-tinged perfume. The way the candlelight danced upon the contours of her bronzed skin beckoned to his senses like the women in white upon the stage who twirled and dipped as they depicted an age-old fertility rite. Caught up in their passionate portrayal, Toni was oblivious to her surroundings. She looked like a woman ripe for seduction.

She'd chosen to wear a simple tank style sun dress that began at the shoulders in light azure and deepened like the night sky into rich midnight blues. Palm tree silhouettes edged the full hem and caught glints of light in a scattering of jet beads. With her hair twisted up in a flower-studded rope, her lovely features were glamorously framed and the long line of her neck was bare. Except for the tiny scratches around the base of her throat. That reminder shocked Zach's musings back to the harsh reality. She wasn't a pretty tourist. She was a target.

Toni gave a start when he took up her hand. The alarm in her gaze eased quickly into a sultry blend of surprise and some more complex emotion he couldn't afford to identify. In the flickering torchlight from the stage, it pooled like rich, romantic fantasies.

She quirked a puzzled smile as he clasped a silver bracelet studded with lapis and malachite on her wrist. "What's this? A gift? I didn't get you anything?"

But oh, such dangerous promises glittered in her liquid stare.

"Consider us engaged."

As her perplexity deepened and her pulse began to quicken within the warm curl of his fingers, he gently turned her hand and directed her attention to the bracelet band.

"There's a transmitter implanted. A kind of panic button with built-in GPS. If we're separated and you need me, you activate it here, at this catch. I'll know you're in trouble. It's for those discretionary or unexpected moments."

She considered the gift with a new understanding. Her tone was dry. "How romantic. Engaged."

He chose to smile rather than to react to her sarcasm. "Without the mess."

"How convenient."

Just then a swooningly handsome Mateo stepped up to the table. He wore traditional Mexican attire heavily trimmed with braid as well as his huge white smile. He bussed a quick kiss on Toni's cheek before addressing the table.

"I hope you all are enjoying the evening." While he listened to the praise of his guests, his hands lingered familiarly on Toni's shoulders. That she didn't seem to mind the possessive gesture triggered an odd disagreeability in Zach Russell. That feeling intensified when their gregarious host leaned down closer until he was cheek to cheek with the woman at his side. Toni's expression said she not only didn't object but that she returned the affections of the courtly Latino.

"Antonia, I've managed to clear my morning to take you shopping at the market in Zihua. It will be just like the adventures we used to have when we were younger." He glanced up to confide in Zach, "We would sneak off to hop a train into the city then explore all the ethnic neighborhoods around Chicago. The only trouble we got into was from her father." A huge grin. "Well, almost."

Zach's gut clenched on the words *sneak* and *trouble,* but Toni was already geared to go.

"That sounds like such fun. It's been forever since we've gone on an adventure."

"Wonderful. I'll pick you up right after breakfast and the two of us—"

"Three of us," Zach corrected quietly.

Mateo turned his scowl from the stoic bodyguard to Toni, demanding a clarification.

"Three of us," she repeated. "Where I go, he goes."

"Really, Antonia, that's not necessary."

"Yes," Zach countered, "it is."

The two men locked stares, Mateo's all passionate objection and Zach's cool certainty.

"The three of us," the younger man conceded at last.

"You're going into the village?" Bryce leaned in excitedly. "Mind if we tag along? We could get some great candids. Not to mention some great deals on silver."

"You're going shopping?" one of the stylists piped up. "We've been to the tourist shops across the street until the ATM went dry for the day, but our money transfers should go through by morning. Mind if we come along, too? We don't know any Spanish." Her heavily outlined blue eyes fluttered at Mateo. "And we could use someone who knows his way around a good bargain."

Mateo sighed and managed a heroically enthusiastic smile. "We'll form our own tour group."

The girls squealed in appreciation and hugged their drunken dates, who by this time were fairly oblivious to everything but their goal of getting lucky.

After a few moments watching the two youthful and overly demonstrative couples indulge in some PG-13 rapidly approaching R interaction, Toni pushed back from the table. The men on either side of her immediately jumped to attention.

"I think I'll go upstairs. This humidity and the tequila are giving me a bit of a headache."

"Oh, honey," Bryce clucked. "Put a cool cloth over those beautiful eyes. We can't have any swelling before tomorrow's shoot."

"Concern noted." She blew her photographer a kiss. "Good night."

The three of them left the crowded festival area and entered the air conditioned welcome of the hotel. Mateo linked his arm through Toni's to edge Zach out of the way. He followed an obliging step behind, his gaze doing a quick point-to-point search of the open atrium.

"Antonia, we've spent no time together," Mateo complained with a petulant purse of his lips. "I had hoped to steal you away so we could talk, just the two of us."

"Mateo, I'd like that, too. I've missed our talks and the way you make me laugh."

He glanced back at their somber shadow. "I could arrange a little escape."

"Russell would not be pleased."

"And since when is pleasing him more important than pleasing me?"

Toni squeezed his arm. "You sound like a jealous suitor."

"Perhaps I am."

Toni chuckled, dismissing the sudden intensity in his expression as pure drama. She touched the bracelet on her wrist, her mood sobering. "You don't have to be jealous of Russell. He doesn't have a personal bone in his body. He's not interested in my heart, only my health."

"Foolish man."

Toni silently agreed.

They reached the bank of glass elevators. One of the desk clerks called to Mateo and held up a phone receiver.

"I have to take that." Mateo hugged her briefly and pressed a kiss to her brow. "Sweet dreams, *novia*."

Toni slipped past Zach into the elevator, moving to the rail and putting her back to him as he pushed for their floor. Fatigue pounded at the base of her skull. An illogical irritation with Russell had that knot of pain fisting tighter.

"Step back from the glass," Russell commanded as they lifted from the lobby and began the upward climb.

Just weary enough to be contentious, she snapped, "I really don't think there's any danger in—"

That's when the elevator shuddered to a stop between floors eight and nine.

Toni gasped as Zach's arm scooped about her middle

to swing her to the back of the car. Pushed back against the doors with Russell's body between her and any potential assailant, Toni felt the first cold spike of terror.

"Stay behind me."

Zach's quiet order froze her in place. While he scanned the open halls that ringed each floor, he pressed the various panel buttons to no avail. Finally, he sounded the alarm bell. As the sharp sound echoed in the elevator, the light suddenly went out.

Toni flattened against the door, her eyes squeezing shut, the breath thickening in her throat. Just a coincidence, she told herself as fear shuddered through her. Russell would never let anything happen to her.

Minutes ticked by as they hung suspended in the darkened cubical. Without air movement, the temperature quickly rose to a stifling degree. But it was cold that wracked Toni's body from head to toe, a deep, deathly chill that had her teeth clattering and her limbs trembling.

"Zach?" Her voice trembled, too.

"It's all right. I'm with you." The calming power of that statement grounded her escalating panic. "Look. There's a security guard with a radio. They'll get us out. Help's on the way. Hang in there."

She nodded and concentrated on breathing.

The light flickered on overhead. Zach concealed the pistol in his hand as the car jerked then began to move upward once more. One, two, three floors then the doors slid open and Toni spilled on nearly boneless legs into the hallway. Zach's palms cupped under her elbows in support but after a few deep draws of air, she was able to push away from him as the security guard emerged from the stairwell.

"Everything all right?"

"Yes. Thank you," she returned in a thready voice.

"It happens sometimes. I apologize for the inconvenience."

"No problem," she assured him with a smile as watery as her knees. She lurched toward their suite, the sweat cold on her face and neck, her heart pounding an anxious rhythm against her ribs. Zach opened the door but had her wait in the alcove until he'd turned on the lights and done a cursory sweep of the interior. When he nodded the all clear, she wobbled across the room and out onto the balcony to suck in the cooler taste of ocean air. Zach turned off the lights behind her so her figure wouldn't be silhouetted against the room's brightness. Though he didn't join her, she could feel him standing just on the other side of the slider's threshold.

The fiesta had broken up below but a different celebration had begun at the resort next to them. A dais surrounded by mock pillars hosted a wedding party with the bride and groom seated in throne-backed rattan chairs while their guests, all in white, line danced to the Spanish rendition of *Achy Breaky Heart*. A poignant smile touched Toni's lips as she watched the revelers far below. She thought of the couples at their table during the fiesta, unashamedly necking, and witnessed the hopefulness of a new beginning in the celebration of dance and music and lantern light below. Personal delights she would never experience. A future she would never have. A bittersweet sigh escaped her as she turned away and was met with the imposing shape of the one man who didn't wake all her defenses.

"You look exhausted. You should take a shower and get some sleep."

"That's a fairly personal observation, Mr. Russell."

"A practical one, Ms. Castillo. But do what you like."

"I'd like to just sit a minute and unwind." The claustro-phobic entrapment in the elevator had unnerved her more than she cared to admit. Just a coincidence. Not a sign that danger had followed her here to this paradise. Perhaps she was being overly sensitive, overly cautious, looking for threat in every shadow, suspicious of every circumstance. Or maybe she wasn't wrong for feeling the stresses con-stantly gnawing just beneath the surface. She didn't have to confess these things to Zach. He knew. And that's why she felt brave enough to take a chance by saying, "Sit with me."

He moved with her to the couch that would become his bed. She sat in the center and after he opened the second slider so the night breeze could filter in, he joined her. For a long moment, they sat in silence, not touching, not ac-knowledging the fact that they were achingly aware of one another just as they had been ten years ago. That it was no less acceptable now than it had been then. Then Toni gave in and made the first move, shifting, leaning so that her head found the strong, inviting angle of his chest and shoulder. He lifted his arm to accommodate her, letting it curve lightly about her back, his hand resting easy upon the back of her head. Words would have ruined the poi-gnant moment so neither spoke. And finally, after long minutes ticked by, Zach felt her relax into a malleable slumber. Only then did he turn his face into the soft cush-ion of her hair to inhale its subtle fragrance.

She didn't deserve the torment the past was putting her through. That was his fault.

If there was any way to lessen her pain, her guilt, her

fear, he swore an oath at that moment when she was vulnerable in his arms, that he would do whatever it took to give her back some sort of normal life.

Whatever it took.

Chapter 8

Tomas picked them up in the hotel limo. After he'd assured Zach that he'd inspected the vehicle as he'd been shown, the shoppers were loaded in and they started up and away from the coastal city. The girls and the two photographers chattered nonstop. The beach boys had passed on the excursion, electing to sleep off the effects of the fiesta at poolside.

In the rear seat, Toni sat wedged between a silent Russell and Mateo, who was actively pointing out the sights as they drove by. Toni wasn't listening. She was pondering the fact that she'd woken up on Zach's sofa, surrounded by his scent and feeling wonderfully refreshed.

Had he held her all night long?

As they approached the village of Zihuatanejo, Bryce rolled down the window to take some shots of the vastly different landscape. Instead of the neat boulevards lined with walled resorts, pharmacias, trendy shops and restaurants beckoning for the tourist dollar, these dilapidated buildings squatted at the roadside, squeezed together in a broken patchwork of brick and uneven corrugated steel, forming a weary pattern of poverty. Beyond that tattered neighborhood, cut into an inhospitable mountainside, were homes, most of them little more than shacks that seemed stuck into the sheer face like precarious push pins.

"How do they get up there?" one of the girls exclaimed in a horrified fascination. "What kind of people can live like that?"

"The ones who serve you your meals, and leave a flower on your turned down bedsheets," Tomas answered without looking back in the rearview. "The ones who check out your beach towels and bring you your poolside drinks. My family."

The only sound after that was the quiet whirring of Bryce's camera as he took candids of the wizened men crouched in front of a graffiti-ridden bar and of the battered pickup trucks they passed with whole families standing up in the open beds to catch the breeze on their way to work in the posh hotels of Ixtapa.

As they entered the village, the quality of the buildings improved, becoming grocery stores, car repair shops, museums and the inevitable tourist shops hawking beach accessories and gaudy tee shirts. Their destination was at the far side of the busy traditional town.

Tomas wheeled them expertly onto a narrow one-way street where every other block was under some sort of construction and the compact cars that lined either side of the road were coated with a patina of grime. He maneuvered around the taxis angled in carelessly at any opening to drop off their neatly dressed foreign passengers and cut in behind a shiny red sports car to let them out.

"Page me when you've had enough," Tomas instructed. He held the door open to the parade of wares dangling beneath an endless canopy of awnings suspended over the sidewalk, offering a hospitable shade under which to spend one's pesos.

The market was a rabbit warren of temporary plank walls on uneven cement and cobbled floors. From their rented booths, the locals offered everything from high quality silver, leather goods, and carved mahogany pieces to tiles and bowls painted with colorful callas and wedding scenes, coaxing the passers-by with claims of "Almost free. Like Kmart." Every available space was hung with woven handbags, string hammocks and never ending tee shirts. The booths went back four to six deep and tourist traffic wound from section to section through narrow aisles heaped with more souvenir treasures.

Toni liked to shop. Despite her inheritance, she had a nose for a bargain and it was twitching at these incomparable deals. Mateo led her back into the merchandise-draped caverns, explaining what stamped number to look for on the silver to tell its purity and negotiating prices for any trinket that caught her eye. Russell followed a few paces behind, carefully staying out of Bryce's viewer, his attention on the crowd rather than the trinkets.

As the morning progressed, the oppressive heat in the crowded marketplace made the tiny cubicles into sweat-boxes. After exclaiming over the seemingly unique items found in the first few aisles, repetition of goods urged Toni to move more quickly than her companions in search of the truly original. She picked up a heavy green glass pyramid to use as a paperweight on her desk, then sorted through her fanny pack when the seller exclaimed, "Not pesos. American dollars." While the weighty souvenir was wrapped in the daily newspaper for travel safety, she noticed a chess set with pieces carved from onyx and quartz. Though her father didn't play, he liked to have items of sophistication scattered about him. Thinking this was the sort of gift he'd enjoy, she asked the teenage boy in charge of the booth to give her a price.

"I'm interested in this chess set, but there's a chip on the queen. Do you have another?"

An older man scurried over grinning obligingly. "*Sí,* lady. You come with me. We have another booth."

Toni glanced about. Mateo was busy helping the girls select beach cover-ups from a suspended ceiling hook. Zach had been cornered by a woman with bundled necklaces of shell, beads and precious stones strung on her arms like leis who was insistent that he choose for his sweetheart, two for ten American dollars. Toni gestured to the next aisle, bringing an immediate furrow to his brow. When she hesitated, her salesman pulled at her arm impatiently, urging, "Lady, you come. I have Mexican air conditioning." He pointed to an old metal fan that ineffectively moved the heavy air. "I have many stones to choose from. You come. No cost to look."

She smiled and allowed herself to be coaxed to the next aisle, trying to keep Zach in sight.

"Lady, you come. Over here."

His pulling became more insistent, moving her beyond the next aisle and down into another. When he towed her across several side passages, she started to balk in earnest.

"My friends," she protested.

"Here, lady."

"Wait."

It was then her other arm was gripped by a rough hand. Something sharp pricked beneath her ribs.

"Walk with us, *señorita*. Do not call for help."

There were different ways to call for help. Toni pressed the catch of her bracelet and walked docilely between the two men. A robbery? A kidnapping? Blood began pounding in her head, making it difficult for her to think. They were pulling her quickly through the maze of corridors. She did her best to slow them without seeming to, stumbling, dragging her feet, until they were off balance struggling to propel her forward. The sudden brilliance as they broke from the shaded aisles and onto the sidewalk was enough to make them hesitate for an instant. But it was long enough.

Toni dipped abruptly to the left then came up swinging the bag that held her glass pyramid. It caught her pseudo-salesman in the temple. He staggered, giving her just enough slack to twist free and bolt out into the street. A horn blared. A cry escaped her as a hand caught her braid, using it to whirl her out of traffic and back up onto the sidewalk. She fell over a basket of papier-mâché parrots but the hold on her hair didn't lessen. As the vendor began shrieking in Spanish, her assailant hauled her toward a battered VW bus that listed wearily at the curb. The utility door was open.

Horrible remembrances flooded back, paralyzing her muscles, numbing her brain, freezing her vocal cords. Her knees buckled, slowing their progress just long enough for a sleek black limo to squeal a sharp U-turn and catapult over the curb, coming between them and the van.

Shocked back into action, Toni jerked free and darted into the caverns of the market, dodging beneath racks of shirts and near motionless wind catchers in an effort to escape her would-be captor. As she slipped through a curtain of shells at a full run, an arm banded her waist, using her momentum to swing her around and behind a solid form just as her pursuer thrust through the wildly swaying strands. Only to skid to a halt with Zach's pistol nearly up his nose.

"Think about it," came his soft warning.

While Toni pressed her face between Zach's shoulder blades, her fingers clenched in his damp linen shirt, the attacker thought better of pursuing his present course of action. He gripped a handful of beaded ropes and jerked hard to bring the curtain, rod and all, down upon them. Zach stepped back, his movement one of instinctive protection instead of pursuit. The man was gone like a hare down a hole.

Pocketing his gun, Zach turned to meet her wide-eyed stare. His hands bolstered her elbows when her legs threatened to give way. "I got your call."

Issuing a shaky laugh, she leaned her forehead against his chest. Fear flooded from her in violent tremors.

"Antonia? What's happened?"

She straightened in time to greet Mateo with a wobbly smile of reassurance. "Someone tried to grab my bags and you know me, I just couldn't let go. Thankfully Russell showed up to break the stalemate."

For once, Mateo let his hostilities go long enough for a sincere, "I am thankful as well. Antonia sometimes does not know when to back down. I am in your debt." He put out his hand.

"That debt's been paid," Zach told him somberly but he took the proffered hand in a firm clasp.

"I think I've had enough shopping for one day," Toni announced. "Mateo, could you see the others get back safely?"

Clearly becoming the shepherd for her friends was not what he had in mind, but Mateo agreed with his own conditions. "If you'll spend some time alone with me this evening."

"Just me and my shadow."

Mateo's smile curled slightly. "Of course."

Tomas was waiting outside the big limo. He'd managed to park it behind the abandoned van and was watching the local police going through it. He offered Toni a smile and handed her the bag she'd used to cold-cock one of her attackers. That man was sitting in the back of the police car with an ice pack pressed to his bloodied temple.

"They said they didn't need this as evidence. No one identified you as the victim."

"Thank you, Tomas." Toni took the bag and cautioned a glance at the man in custody. "Did he say if it was a robbery attempt?"

"He's said nothing, Miss Castillo. The van was stolen and his friend is long gone."

Zach held the door to the limo open for Toni, eager to get her off the street and out of sight before some witness came forward to link her to the activity. After she was inside, he turned to the young driver. "Antonia tells me that was some pretty fancy defensive driving for a city chauffeur."

Tomas smiled somewhat sheepishly. "I went to a rather

exclusive school for training. Jack Chaney sends his regards. He thought you might need some assistance."

"Did he now?" Good old Jack. Always one step ahead.
"Then see if you can arrange for me to talk to our mate
after he's booked. I'd rather like to know what was on his
mind." He slipped Tomas a thick wad of currency and
joined Toni in the backseat.

Zach was still shaking inside.

When he'd looked up from the squat little woman trying to sell him necklaces, Toni was gone.

At that moment, Zach Russell had realized that Rule
Three no longer applied to Antonia Castillo. There was
nothing even remotely professional about the icy terror so-
lidifying in his belly when he couldn't find her. He'd run
from corridor to corridor. No sign of her. Panic seized
control of his rational thought process.

Then his pocket locator beeped and all his honed instincts had jumped into play.

Now she was sitting next to the far door, her face turned
slightly away from him so he couldn't quite discern her
mood.

If anything had happened to her...

"Do you think it was a robbery?"

Her voice was quiet but sounded in control.

"Perhaps."

"Perhaps not. Random or planned, do you think?"

"It doesn't matter. It's not my job to solve crimes, just
to prevent them."

She nodded once. His response was a cop-out. True, but
a cop-out nonetheless. Though she didn't say it, her stiff
body language conveyed that message loud and clear.

"When does Premiero arrive?"

"In two days. Why? Do you want to lock me in the suite until then?" A bit more tartness to her tone. That was good.

"If I thought you'd stay put."

Locked in a suite with Antonia Castillo for two days…and nights…presented other dangers.

Tomas sank behind the wheel. As he adjusted the rear-view mirror, he nodded to Zach.

The ride back to the hotel was silent and pensive. Both were thinking along the same line.

Random or planned?

Watching her, one would never know of the morning's trauma.

Zach sat beneath a shading palm-frond umbrella, nursing a bottled water, while the subject of his scrutiny played beach volleyball on a patch of wetted-down sand.

She was gorgeous. A fit, healthy female animal, bronzed by the sun and gleaming with exertion. Instead of the teeny weeny bikinis worn by most of the women, she chose one of the suits from the Aletta line to accentuate her curves. The black-and-white high-cut bottom featured a wide hip-hugging waistband, and the cropped tank-style top provided support while making an eye-popping statement, proving more was sometimes…more. And, of course, she wore the shoes for the benefit of Bryce's camera.

The game went on for over an hour in the broiling sun with Toni playing hard, but relaxed and laughing often. The way it should be instead of the tightly strung, nervous woman he'd returned to the hotel late that morning. If it had been in his power, fear would never shadow her lovely blue eyes again. If he did his job right, perhaps this would be true. He did another scan of the area, noting the faces, the positioning of everything and everyone from poolside bunnies to drink carrying servers, looking for a potential threat. Anyone could conceal a gun. But he didn't think this was about getting off a clean shot. This was about down and dirty intimidation. This was more personal than professional. Someone knew the secret horrors of Toni's past and was using them to terrorize her. But for what purpose? Who would benefit from Antonia Castillo's fear?

He glanced up at Tomas's approach. In shorts and a tank top, the young Latino looked more like a guest than a hired driver. Or a government operative.

"News?"

"He's got some high-profile lawyer flying in from Mexico City this afternoon. Once he gets here, our friend will be gone."

"Any chance of getting a private word with him before that happens?"

"Could be. I have a cousin who works in the jail. If you are there and the men assigned to him just happen to take a break." He shrugged meaningfully.

"Can you take me there?"

"Can you leave now?"

Zach's attention shifted back to the beach then to the pool. "Give me a minute."

Veta Chavez sat stretched out in a lounger, her face and the political thriller she was reading shaded by a huge brimmed straw hat. There was a tin bucket next to her chair with the remains of two Mexican beers and a dish of squeezed lime wedges. She looked every inch the leisurely tourist until that brim lifted to reveal the all-business directness of her gaze. Zach posed his request.

"I need you to fill in for me."

* * *

Toweling the sweat from her face and shoulders, Toni searched the sea of white chaises, but it was Veta who waved her over, not Zach.

"Where's Russell?" After the morning's excitement, his absence upset Toni more than his always aggravating presence.

Veta put down her book and passed her friend a cold drink from her newly refilled bucket. "He said he had something to do. Could you settle for me this afternoon?"

"Gladly." She dropped into the adjoining couch and took a long swallow of the golden beer.

"Mateo told me what happened this morning," Veta began. She skewered Toni with a probing stare. "He doesn't think it was a purse snatching and neither do I. This is the second time someone's gotten past Russell. What good is he if he can't protect you?"

How to explain the good Zach's mere presence did for her peace of mind?

"Both times were my fault. I broke the rules."

"Rules." Veta made a rude noise. "Toni, you need a professional to take care of your interests and those of Aletta. This is a dangerous place. Teo tells me executives get snatched off the street all the time and held for ridiculous ransoms. We already know your father's response to such a thing. If something happens to you, could Aletta pay the price for your return and still prosper?"

Toni's blood chilled. "What do you mean?"

"Could we afford to pay a ransom without bankrupting the company?"

A tremor started deep in Toni's belly. "Russell won't let anything happen to me."

"Things happen, Toni. You've got to protect yourself and your future. Your father's not going to. And Russell hasn't done a very good job so far."

In her mind's eye, she saw the van's sliding utility door standing open and the darkness waiting inside.

When Toni hesitated, Veta continued in earnest. "Mateo wants you to meet with someone. He insures wealthy executives against the possibility of kidnapping. The premium is staggering but the benefits far outweigh that. If something happens to you, these people step in to do the negotiating. They pay the ransom demand and take all the risks."

No. Toni knew better than that. She'd still be taking all the risks.

"Think about it, Antonia. Just a temporary policy while you're in this country. Don't let your father be in control of your safety."

And suddenly, even with the tropical sun beating down on her, Toni felt cold to the very marrow.

His conversation with Toni's would-be assailant was a dead end. Zach's money bought him five minutes alone with the supremely self-confident thug who refused to say anything until his lawyer arrived. His story would be that he merely tried to help some *Americano* woman who misinterpreted his intentions. And he got ten stitches in his brow for his troubles. And if that wasn't the truth, where was the supposed victim who would challenge his fairy tale?

Toni wouldn't come forward to press charges. She wouldn't risk the negative publicity such a thing would bring to the Aletta merger and apparently, this uneducated street punk knew that or he wouldn't be calmly smoking a cigarette in defiance of Zach's best intimidation.

Such confidence and knowledge didn't come cheap. Whoever paid the two locals to grab Antonia Castillo knew the target and knew what her reaction would be.

Zach left the station, disheartened until he saw the private car pull up out front, announcing the arrival of the high-priced criminal lawyer. Zach looked to the young supposed driver leaning patiently against his own transportation.

"Tomas, how much trouble would it be to find out who this dirt bag represents?"

"A phone call or two. Or just open the local paper. His main client is Angel Premiero."

Premiero. Sitting in the front seat of the limo next to Tomas, Zach considered it on the ride back to the Royale.

"What's Premiero's connection to Castillo? Not the official version but the behind the scenes."

Tomas was silent for a moment, weighing his answer and how much he should reveal. "They grew up together here in Mexico. They ran the streets playing shill games with tourists and getting into trouble with the policia. Castillo was the smarter, the slicker of the two and he found a way out by finding a sponsor in America, by going to night classes and by marrying well. Premiero made enough money to dress in imported suits and have fine things but he will always be little more than a knee breaker on Castillo's payroll."

Was he still or had he moved up in the world to do the dirty work for his own benefit?

"Making Mercedes Aletta his wife took Castillo out of the gutter and into a whole new social registry. Premiero had to resent him for that." Tomas continued. "You can take the man off the streets, but you take those years on the streets out of the man. They are cut from the same crude cloth. And now Premiero wants to start playing in the same exclusive league as his childhood amigo." Tomas pointed to a gap between the high-rise hotels. Only a burned out shell remained. "Castillo's. Some say Premiero is responsible. Some say he did it for revenge. Some say he did it for a friend."

And this was the man Toni was going into partnership with. The man she was going to trust with her mother's legacy.

Was she crazy? Or was she well aware that she was getting into bed with the devil?

It was late when he got back to the hotel. The sun was already setting. In a hurry to find Toni and secure his place at her side, he headed for the elevator and a change of clothes only to be hailed by the desk clerk. He took the telegram, noting its origin in Detroit. Jack. He tore into it in the elevator, scanning the message that brought another possible player to the forefront of his suspicions. One he didn't like to consider.

The suite was empty. Toni's swimsuit hung in the tub. Zach stepped out onto the balcony to scan the pool area below. It was mostly empty except for couples crossing the lighted cement bridge that spanned the two sections of the pool as they headed for a walk along the beach or a drink at the open-air restaurant. At one of the restaurant tables, a woman sat alone. The dramatic hat was unmistakable.

Veta raised her glass to him as Zach approached. "You look like you could use one of these."

"Where's Toni?"

Veta didn't react to the menace in his tone. "She's fine."

"That doesn't answer my question."

Veta pointed outward. He looked past the middle aged man watching his children weave in and out of the incoming surf to where the horizon was a smudge of blue sky at the edge of grey seas. Graceful sails glided along that melding of air into water.

"Don't worry. She's in good hands. She's with Mateo."

Zach took no comfort from that claim.

Toni was out on the ocean with a man who may have had every reason to harm her.

Chapter 9

It should have been a relaxing moment in paradise. The eighty-five-foot windjammer schooner glided across the twilight waters. The breeze filling the parade of canvas was warm yet wonderfully refreshing. Seated on the open deck with the blackness of the Pacific behind them and the twinkling of the hotel zone lining the distant beach, a handsome, adoring man beside her and a starry canopy overhead to wish on, another woman would have been swept up in the romance. Antonia Castillo was brokering a business deal.

"You won't regret it, Toni. It's the closest thing to a guarantee of safety I know."

She nodded absently at Mateo's words as her new insurance representative folded the paper with her signature and tucked it into his briefcase. Mateo had arranged the discreet meeting between them. The modestly dressed and properly mannered salesman had all the references to make her feel secure and in good hands. So why did she feel as if those hands had just pulled out of her pockets after giving her a good fleecing?

The seeping sense of uneasiness didn't leave along with her bankcard number when the impeccably dressed insurance agent went below deck. Toni knew she'd done the right thing for Aletta. And that was the important thing, that Aletta go on.

"Thank you for setting this up for me, Mateo."

"I would do anything for you, Toni. You know that. I know how much your mother's company means to you. I only wish I could be as important in your life."

She thought he was teasing at first. It wasn't like Mateo to speak with any seriousness about his emotions, but when she glanced at him, beginning to smile, she saw a sobering truth in his dark eyes. And the heat of an underlying hope.

Why hadn't she seen this coming? When had Mateo's feelings for her matured from childhood friendship into an adult devotion?

"Don't be silly, Mateo. Aletta is just a thing. You've been like family for most of my life. Like my brother and my best friend."

He made a regretful face. "Just what a man wants to hear when he's out on the ocean with the most beautiful woman in the world."

"And what did you expect to hear?" She kept a teasing tone in her voice to lessen whatever he was leading up to.

"That you've missed me. That you've thought of me often."

"Those things are true."

"Then why do I hear what's happening to you from my sister instead of from you?"

"What's Veta told you?"

"That you've been threatened. That your father is pushing this deal with Premiero even though you're not sure it's the right thing for Aletta. Or for you. That you're all work and no play and you've forgotten how to have fun."

"I just needed you to remind me."

"Maybe you need me for more than just an occasional phone call. I'm here for you. I always have been."

"I know."

"You were the one watching my back and cleaning up after my mistakes as we were growing up. You protected me from those who would take advantage of my foolishness by paying off my debts. I want to do the same for you."

"You think I'm being foolish?"

"I think you're in more trouble than you'll admit. And you're scared and alone. Let me help you, Toni. Let me be more than a friend."

In her heart, she knew what he was suggesting but if she acknowledged it, she was afraid everything about their relationship would change and her best friend in the world would be gone. Before she could think of a way to forestall it, he said the words.

"I love you, Toni."

"I love you, too."

He frowned because the words were the ones he wanted to hear but the significance of them was underplayed. "As a friend and a brother."

"Always."

"How about as a partner. A life partner. One who can protect you and make you laugh."

"Is that what you want to do?"

"If it's all you'll let me do. Toni, I know what happened to you. I know why you've never gotten serious or close to any man."

She froze. All the playfulness and gentle feelings went overboard as her innate defensiveness seized up inside her chest.

"Veta told you?"

"She didn't have to. You've never been the same since then. And I blame your father and his greed."

"I don't want to talk about this."

He tried to take up her hand but she jerked it away. She couldn't help herself.

"Toni, you don't have to be alone. Let me take care of these things for you like you've taken care of me in the past. I can take the heat from your father and Premiero. I can step out front so that you don't have to be the target of intimidation. You'll be free to do the work that you want to do with the company. I can take the pressure off. Let me take the risks. All you have to do is say yes."

"Yes to what?"

"Marry me, Antonia. Together we can take them all on and win."

"Mateo—"

Hearing the objection and reluctance in her voice, he pushed his case. "It can be on whatever terms you want it to be. As friends, to start. As partners. You don't have to take on the world by yourself. Let me help you, Toni. Say yes and I can make all the nightmares go away."

She stared up at him in confusion. In some corner of her mind, she was actually playing the possibilities, considering his offer.

Until he bent down, thinking to kiss her.

Two things were immediately apparent when Toni opened the door to the suite. Zach was furious. And he was packing. He gave her a quick look before continuing to fold his shirts. Anger radiated from him, not in gestures or attitude but in the complete absence of expression. She might well not have been in the room.

She stood just inside the door for a long moment, following his precise movements as the realization of what he was doing kept building and building.

He was leaving her.

Faced with the choice of a defensive or offensive approach, Toni went with the latter. She sighed heavily and when she spoke, her tone was an impatient mix of irritation and weariness.

"I'm not in the mood for this, Russell. Not after the day I've had."

He paused long enough to draw a slow, stabilizing breath. Still he wouldn't acknowledge her with his full attention. "You're not in the mood. Fancy that. We're finally in agreement on something."

To her dismay, he reached for another shirt and began to make meticulous folds. Anxiety massing until she found it difficult to swallow, Toni finally crossed the room, her alarm making her more aggressive and short tempered.

"Stop the game, Russell. Just spank me with your lecture about the rules so I can get to sleep. I'm tired."

He did look at her then and his chilled gaze was the darkly shadowed green of the surrounding jungle, filled with dangers and pitfalls untold. His accent thickened along with his ire. "I'm tired, too. Tired of the games, especially the kind you were playing tonight. If you can't take your protection seriously, the joke's on you, Ms. Castillo. I told you quite plainly what would happen if you refused to accept my terms."

"And so now you're punishing me for my disobedience by making this dramatic gesture."

"No. You're the expert there. I don't make threats, Toni, and I don't make deals and I don't make fools out of those who are hired to take care of my interests."

"I ditched you and it hurt your feelings?"

"My feelings don't matter one way or another."

"That's right. You'd have to have them first, wouldn't you."

"Oh, I have them. I wish to God I didn't because I don't ever want to have to feel what I did ten years ago when the call came to say you were gone." He placed his shirt in the open case, stacking it neatly atop the others.

Recklessly, Toni plunged on. "So this is about your professional pride? You're afraid I'll make another black mark on your record."

"I'm afraid they'll be zipping you up in a black plastic bag because you just can't seem to help throwing yourself from one bad situation to another."

"The only bad thing I've ever thrown myself at is you. And we know how that turned out, don't we?"

Calmly, with enviable control, Zach closed the lid to his suitcase. "This isn't going to work, Toni. I knew it was a bad idea from the start."

"Bad ideas and bad situations. That's all we have between us, isn't it, Russell?"

He regarded her impassively. "That and bad company."

"Mateo? Is this about Mateo?" The wild notion that he might be somehow jealous went to her head like a snort of pure oxygen. But she quickly shook it off. This was Russell, after all, and he would never let emotions cloud the issue. "I was perfectly safe with him. There's no reason for you to react like this."

"You're so sure of that, are you?"

"He asked me to marry him."

Zach blinked. "Congratulations." He turned to zip the suitcase. The sound was harsh, like their inevitable parting. After a beat, he asked, "What did you tell him?"

When she didn't reply right away, he was forced to look at her again. The depths of his forest gaze were filled with unpredictable shadows.

Her answer was unsparingly blunt. "I told him no, that I was no bargain, that I came with too much baggage to ever be a bride."

Zach stared at her for a long, impassive moment then made an uncharitable sound. "What a crock. And he believed you? The man's an idiot."

"No. He's a good man and he's my friend. He deserves better than—than a woman who can't bear a man's touch. And we both know why, don't we?"

She could only imagine what he'd seen when he opened that cellar door to find her huddled, bound, bleeding and naked on the dirty floor of her prison. It had taken him only two days to locate her once the ransom had been refused. But those two days had been filled with a spirit-scarring hell. When he'd stripped off her blindfold, she'd been close to catatonic from the abuse she'd suffered. Abuse no woman should be made to suffer. Especially when it was her first time.

He knew it was, because when he'd gathered her up into a tender embrace, his coat bundled about her to hide her shame, she'd clung to him about the neck, to whisper words that burned to his soul.

"It should have been you. I wanted you to be my first."

But first times never happened more than once, and the chance for her to learn about intimacy between a man and a woman the way it was meant to be was lost to her forever.

She picked up the suitcase and swung it behind her. "Don't go, Russell."

He reached for the bag, but that brought him into sudden close proximity to her. He froze. Her eyes were huge seas of blue, shimmering like the ocean at sunrise, liquid, salty, beckoning. But those tears didn't fall.

Her voice when she spoke was rough with forced sincerity.

"Do you want me to beg you?"

Horrified by the very idea, he took a step back, increasing the distance as if that would automatically guarantee a measure of safety. But he didn't count on her taking a matching step forward.

"I will, you know. I'm not very good at it. I haven't had much practice."

"Don't do this, Toni." He put out his hands to keep her back but the feel of her bare upper arms, all smooth silky skin over surprisingly hard muscle, only made things worse. Only made things more real and more immediate.

"Don't leave, Russell. I need you."

He argued the point on the only linear level he understood as a man. "*Why?* You won't listen to me. You won't do what I tell you. You won't follow the simple precautions required to keep you safe. I can't do you any good if you won't let me do my job. Why did you hire me if you have no intentions of playing by my rules?"

"You're the only man I trust, the only one I can let close to me."

"You didn't seem to be having any trouble where your friend Chavez was concerned. Or with any of those pretty, muscle-bound fellows who seem to keep you company in the tabloids." How petty and unprofessional that sounded. It surprised both of them into a moment's silence.

Only then did Toni find the courage to explain.

"I have lots of men who are my friends. Men who'll share drinks and swap stories, who'll race me in fast cars and on fast bikes, who'll show me how to change out plugs or field dress an elk, who'll spar with me in a boxing ring or on a judo mat. I don't have any problems with men as friends, as competitors, as teachers, as business partners. As long as they treat me as an equal and with respect. As long as they don't…as long as they don't try to get close."

He understood then. And he started to remove his hands from her arms. She dropped his suitcase and seized his wrists, holding him in place, keeping him from retreating.

He went very still.

"Russell, I'm a prisoner inside my own life."

With a quiet candor, he told her, "Get help, Toni. All you have to do is ask for it."

She moved closer, pushing against the resistance in his

arms, leaning toward him, toward the answer she needed to hear.

"I'm asking. *Help me, Zach.*"

Chapter 10

His answer was painfully blunt.

"Are you asking me to take you to bed?"

Controlling her frustration and embarrassment with obvious difficulty, she told him, "To bed, to the couch, to the shower, on the floor. I don't care. Just take me away from this dark place I'm in. I asked you once, Zach. Do you remember?"

He closed his eyes tightly but he couldn't shut out the memory of her ragged voice.

I wanted you to be the first.

"Do you want me to beg you now? I will. I have no more pride. I can't go on like this, being separate from the world, afraid of a simple touch, of living a normal life. I don't want to be alone, Zach. I can't cry. Since you found me, I've never been able to cry. I want to *feel* something, something that's not fear, something that's not panic. I'll never be strong. I'll never be in control. I'll never be able to be…happy. Put aside your rules this once. If you have any feelings for me at all." Then a sharp spear of memory brought back his phone call to another woman. She spoke through a painful cramp in her throat. "Unless there's someone else."

He was motionless for a long, agonizing moment. His features seemed set in stone.

"Zach?"

He took a breath and the facade began to crumble. "No."

"No, what?" The raw hurting in her voice forced his answer.

"Oh, bloody hell." He spoke the curse with a soft reverence, the words as gentle as the touch he brushed along the side of her pale cheek. "No one else."

She closed her eyes on a sigh and turned her head slightly to press her lips to his palm.

And he was lost. Damn the rules.

She let him draw her to him without resistance. The curl of his arms flattened her to the wall of his chest, his embrace firm, solid yet at the same time, nonthreatening. And he just held her, giving the skittering doubts and residuals of panic time to settle down. Time to let awareness of him build until the steady rhythm of his heartbeat and rock of his breathing became as regular and inviting as the tide of her emotions.

She had wanted him, wanted this for so long. Finally the tangling chaos of her fears relented so she could remember just how much. The ache of it clenched like a fist in her belly, tightening there until the slow stroke of his hand through her hair excited a series of fierce, needy tremors.

Mistaking the cause of her trembling, he hesitated but only until she lifted her head. Her eyes glittered like hot blue flame.

"Make love to me, Zach."

Wordlessly, he led her, not to the bed, not to the couch, but to one of the big overstuffed chairs. He sank down in it, putting his feet up on the footstool while maneuvering Toni to straddle his lap. Perplexed by his odd choice of setting, she let her hands rest lightly on his broad shoulders. Her confusion woke a small smile from him.

"If you want to stop, there's nothing holding you."

In the well-lit room, with nothing to restrict her movements or weight her down, the choice would be hers. There'd be no fighting her way free if she became uncomfortable. She'd be in complete control.

Shaken by his consideration for her fragile state, Toni overcame the sudden paralyzing thickness in her throat by leaning down to kiss him. His mouth was warm and surprisingly yielding to her first innocent forays, parting, inviting her to trust him with more of herself. Curious and flushed with a new increasing confidence, she slipped between his lips, to touch, to taste, to boldly explore, teasing his tongue into a light play that was all hot, wet silk and edgy excitement. She relaxed the cramp of her fingers, letting them knead his shoulders and upper arms instead, reveling in the hard swells and powerful contours until she grew restless with the fabric that kept her from experiencing him more completely. She rocked back, breathing in quick, shallow little pants while her fingers hurried down the buttons of his shirt. He watched her, expression impassive, as she pushed the linen from his shoulders and bared his torso. Her touch trembled down his chest to the sculpted cut of his abdomen.

"You're amazing." Her voice had a rough, velvety catch. "What did you do to build a body like this?"

"I was an Olympic diver during my years at the university. Ranked twelfth in the world. Not so impressive, really."

That would explain the tapered physique and brutally chiseled musculature. Her laugh quavered. "I'm impressed." Her palms smoothed over the defined ridges. "Bryce's camera lens would have a field day."

"I'd prefer Bryce not have a field day with any part of my anatomy, thank you very much. Not in my job description."

"I think your resume needs updating. I can see our next billboard campaign right here."

"For your eyes only, darling."

Even though he spoke teasingly, his words triggered a tigerish possessiveness in Toni. Her fingernails scraped along the sides of his ribs, startling a jerk and tensing of his middle.

"I'm fine with that," she purred, sinking back onto his mouth for more enthusiastic tongue tangoing. Finally, out of breath, her pulse going like crazy, Toni leaned her head upon his shoulder, hoping to recoup some degree of sanity.

But that wasn't Zach's plan.

His thumb charted the bold angle of her cheekbone before hooking beneath her chin. He challenged her with a kiss that escalated from throating-aching tenderness to rampaging hunger. With an intensity that staggered her senses and sent wild, fluttery shocks to waken every extremity. She clung to him, swamped by sensation, her body ripe and throbbing with the need for more…more everything. And all he'd done so far was kiss her!

She sat back, a mass of quivering nerve endings, emotions raw and so vulnerable unshed tears spiked her lashes as they flickered shut. Her voice was husky with impatience when she realized he was waiting for her next cue before proceeding.

"Touch me, Zach."

Her thighs clenched over his as his palms pushed upward, lifting the floating hem of her short sun dress until it pooled over his wrists and left the tiny triangle of her string bikini panties exposed to his view. She drew a ragged breath as his thumbs centered on the moist scrap of nylon to press and circle with maddening insistence, coaxing, then demanding a response from her dormant senses. Building, building. And when those long-starved sensations reached a spectacular completion, her pleasure was voiced in a roar, not a whimper.

She said his name with an explosive gusto, her thighs clamping his, her fingers knotting behind his neck as her body was ravaged by a seismic pleasure. Aftershocks seemed to go on forever until finally, she exhaled raggedly and slumped upon his chest. He stirred a soft murmur of contentment as he rubbed the tension from her back.

"I found that very impressive," he whispered into the flyaway wisps of hair that had escaped the regimented twists of her braid.

"Amazing," she concurred.

After a brief moment to recuperate, Toni sat back to regard him with an endearing shyness.

"You don't have anywhere you have to be, do you?"

"Where you go, I go."

Her fingertip touched to the solemn set of his mouth.

"Then if we're to follow the rules, you have to come with me, Russell."

His eyes glinted dangerously. "We can't break the rules, now can we?"

"Certainly not. And as a professional, I'm sure you've considered every aspect of personal protection."

A smile flirted across his lips. He lifted one hip to pull his wallet from his pants pocket, taking a moment to extract a flat packet. "One must prepare for any eventuality."

"A commendable motto," she agreed, reaching for his zipper.

If she was going to balk, it would be at the moment his engorged sex rocketed free of its confines, aggressive, full and proud. She stared at his impressive maleness, her expression complex, intense and focused inward. Then, with an agony of gentleness, she touched him only to laugh nervously at his twitch of response.

He was studying her features, trying to read reluctance or fear in her wide gaze. "The occasion requires an topcoat. Do you want to do the honors or shall I?"

She realized he was discussing the foil wrapper and chose that moment to plunge ahead with this baptism by fire.

"I will."

She took the packet from him and removed the necessary outerwear. She glanced at the wrapper.

"Extra large. Do you suppose any man would ever go up to the counter and request a small or medium?"

He grinned wide and wolfishly. "They don't come one size fits all. Believe me, love, I plan to rise to the occasion."

And he did even as she rolled the latex down to glove

him. Feeling him pulse hot and hard within her palm got her anticipating how he was going to feel inside her. Where she'd only experienced pain and humiliation before. But that had been in a world that was dark and cold and bereft of all else. And here, with Zach, it was anything but. Sensations ran riotous, varied, hot and inclusive. And she was a full participant. Eager to get beyond the harsh barrier memory had built to explore unknowns that yet teased her nerve endings with tiny shocks of delight. There was so much more she needed to experience. Was ready to experience.

Zach gently but firm urged her to lessen her adoring grip, saying, "It's not wise to give Huey too much encouragement. We wouldn't want him to jump the gun, so to speak."

"Huey?"

"Part of me mum's family is from Louisiana and they were fanatic about politics."

She frowned a moment then grinned at the allusion to Huey Long. "Well, let's not keep the governor waiting."

"Shall we adjourn to more comfortable chambers?" He nodded toward the bed.

"Here's fine. For now."

"Outstanding."

While she gripped his shoulders to keep her balance atop his thighs, Zach skimmed her dress up over her head then tossed it free. The sight of Antonia Castillo in her lacy white undergarments against all that bronzed, smooth and temptingly ample flesh had his heart ricocheting off his ribs. He'd seen her pictured in scanty athletic wear, had observed her emerging from the pool in a wet cling of spandex but this, this was different, this eyes only, intimate view. He drew a deep, tight-chested breath, uncertain of where to start. He didn't want the sudden unexpected unsteadiness of his hands to alarm her with their clumsiness.

Taking advantage of his indecision, Toni undid the back of her bra and shimmied out of it. After holding the cups up to protect her nakedness in a moment of discomfort, she finally let them fall away so Zach could look his fill.

She was used to men ogling her breasts. She'd been early to develop and had always felt awkward with the difference her shape placed between her and her peers. As she matured, she learned to be proud of her healthy physique, but the undue attention to her chest still made her uneasy.

Zach was staring into her eyes, not at her bosom. He held her gaze as he drew her to him for a long, languid kiss. When her muscles had gone to a buttery consistency, his mouth shifted from her lips, to the side of her throat. Tracing the pattern of abuse that still remained. Her fingers locked behind his head as her neck arched, offering that slender curve. And when his head dipped lower, she found it impossible not to respond to the slow drag of his lips around to the underswell of her left breast where he had to be able to taste the thunder of her heartbeats. Her breath caught as his tongue moved in ever tightening circles until her nipple was pebbled with anticipation. She gasped at the brief pull of his mouth. Then trembled fiercely with unrequited need when he moved on to bestow an equally frustrating tender torture upon the other side.

By the time he released the satin strings that tied her panties together, a savage, instinctual kind of wanting possessed her. A desperate wanting to be possessed by him. She drank greedily from his mouth, lifting, poised with the slightest hesitation before sinking onto him.

It was surprise more than any discomfort that had her crying out as she stretched to receive him. Zach's gaze held hers, intent and absorbing. And then she moved and the exquisite friction had her eyes glazing. The ecstasy of sensation only got bigger and bolder as she rose and fell upon him. Pursuing pleasure so raw and sweet it wrung her soul, Toni forgot all that came before and lost herself in the moment. Lost herself to the swirl of sensations that taunted her to the limit before letting go in a series of spirit-cleansing spasms. Shaking her free of the shackling past.

And as those tremors coursed through her, she rode out the sudden harsh surge of Zach's release. Nothing, nothing ever had satisfied so completely.

In a state of wonderful bonelessness, Toni collapsed upon his chest, nestling beneath his stubbled chin. The thunder of his pulse made her smile through her film of exhaustion. Finally, she'd shaken him from his complacency.

As she burrowed against him, there wasn't a calm or controlled fiber in Zach's entire being. Though his body enjoyed a heavy lethargy and his chest plugged solid with tenderness, there was no relief from the sense of contrition gnawing at his mind.

If he'd allowed this to happen ten years ago, he could have spared her a decade of unimaginable pain.

And now that it had happened, how was he going to shift their relationship back into professional mode so he could keep her safe from threats closer to her heart than she realized? Now that passion was no longer the issue, would she demand romance as well? How could he make her understand that he couldn't afford to drop his guard and indulge their emotions while danger yet courted her?

Her lips moved lazily against the side of his neck and he couldn't seem to breathe around the sudden fullness in his throat. He gave himself a few precious minutes to absorb the feel of her against him, upon him. He rubbed his palms over the satiny contours from strong shoulders and narrow waist to the ultrafeminine flare of her hips. The wad of emotion intensified. She was perfection. She was all he'd imagined since the moment he first saw her. And so much more. She embodied everything noble and courageous and admirable. And she didn't deserve less than his best. And that's what she'd get if his loyalties were divided between heart and mind.

"It's late."

He spoke quietly so as not to jar her too rudely from her deliciously languid pose. He felt her go still. He could sense her confusion as she tried to puzzle out his mood. Would she react the way the impetuous teen had done with angry tears and recriminations? With rebellion and recklessness? Had he just complicated the situation beyond repair?

Toni sat back. The sight of her with her tousled hair and kiss-swollen lips staggered his senses. She observed him for a long moment, reading the deliberate and distancing intention in his lack of response. And he realized then that she was no longer that petulant child who thought of nothing beyond her own immediate wants as she dragged up a smile that nailed him squarely in the heart.

"That was truly above and beyond the call, Russell."

She followed that candid critique with a slow, soul-searing kiss that wrapped around his senses before he had time to guard against it. When she eased back, taking his breath and his self-control with her, she was the one to end all thought of foolish fantasy with her bittersweet smile.

"Thank you, Zach."

He sat, stunned into immobility, while she pressed a quick conciliatory peck on his cheek and slid off his lap. As she walked to the bathroom, her stride packed with its usual self-assurance, gloriously unashamed of her own gleaming nakedness, Zach was the one left with his soul rawly exposed.

It took every scrap of his will not to pursue her and all the things promised in the sassy sway of her hips.

He hauled up a breath through the knot in his throat.

See what happens when you break the rules?

What the hell was he going to do about Antonia Castillo?

The lights were out in the living area when Toni finished her long steamy shower. The moonlight whispering in through the parted balcony curtains created a soft glow and revealed everything she needed to know.

The couch was pulled out with Zach's figure mounding the covers in the middle of the mattress. She knew he wasn't sleeping. She could feel the intensity of his stare as he waited to see what she'd do. Agonizing seconds ticked by while she considered the possibilities the way she'd examine the alternate outcomes of a new merger.

If Zach had wanted the intimacies to continue, he would have been waiting in her bed. But then, after weighing the consideration and tenderness he'd shown earlier not to pressure her, not to rush or crowd or frighten her, perhaps this was his way of leaving things yet again in her court.

Or not.

She switched off the bathroom light and stood in the doorway, at the crossroads of this potential relationship.

If she dropped her towel and crossed to the sofa, would he deny her access to his private space? Probably not. But would she be forcing an issue he wasn't ready for or interested in dealing with?

The thought of joining him beneath those covers, fitting close to those amazing contours, to sleep in the security of his embrace... It was almost worth the risk.

Almost.

What he'd gifted her with tonight was immeasurable. He'd allowed her to explore and experience and reap the beauty of a physical union. She'd asked and he'd answered beyond her wildest hopes, creating a safe environment in which to realize the freedom of fulfillment. Her body still hummed with the honey-sweet pleasures they'd shared. The desire to feel those luxurious sensations again was already an addictive craving. As was her desire for Zach Russell.

But what was he feeling? What moved behind those penetrating eyes with the precision of a mainframe computer?

She understood business. She understood power and control. But she hadn't the slightest clue when it came to unlocking the emotions of another, especially when that other was as complex as a time lock at the Federal Reserve.

She'd asked him to release her from her fears and he had. He'd begun the process of her healing. It was up to her now to build upon the confidence he'd bestowed upon her. It wouldn't be fair to demand more. Especially if he was motivated by guilt. The last thing she wanted was his sacrifice.

She'd demanded it of him once. She'd looked up at him, her savior, her will crushed, her body brutally betrayed, and she'd pleaded for his mercy.

Please don't let anyone ever know how you found me.

And he hadn't. Even Veta, who'd come so quickly upon the scene after she'd shot and killed her fleeing attacker, was kept from the truth. After a time, she'd guessed, but that knowledge hadn't come from Zach Russell, who'd quickly and efficiently covered up the crime done against her. No police were called in. Castillo made sure his agency buried the event so it would never make its way to the press. She'd promised Zach as he left her at her father's door that she would make sure no lasting damage had been done. He'd kept his promise much better than she had her own. His way of handling his oath was to shoulder the brunt of responsibility without flinching. Hers was to hide the truth and her shame where it continued to fester to this very day.

Though Zach Russell might think he owed her a debt, the reverse was true. Now, more than ever.

Braced by the thought of his remorse and his willingness to assuage it with the remedy she'd offered, Toni turned to her own bed and solitary covers.

If there was something beyond obligation to Zach's fantastic sexual tutelage, she would find out before pursuing further intimacies. She'd told him she had no pride left. That wasn't quite true, she discovered as she determinedly closed her eyes and tried to shut out the awareness of her every desire just a room length away.

Chapter 11

One more day until Angel Premiero's arrival would change Toni from model to CEO and nothing was going right.

A black flag fluttering on the beach signaled water too rough for a majority of what they had planned. Then it looked as though the poolside shots for the new swimsuit line would be canceled because the male model they'd hired had spent the evening indulging at Señor Frog's with several underage girls. There was nothing attractive about the bruised ribs from a bar fight and broken blood vessels in his pretty face as a result of praying into the porcelain bowl in his room for the better part of the early-morning hours.

Toni paced the pool area, a massive headache beginning to build from too much coffee and a gnawing tension. She was very aware of Zach off to one side doing his best to look inconspicuous as he read the local morning edition from a chaise lounge. Behind his dark glasses, she was sure his gaze never touched upon any of the column inches. He was scanning the crowd drawn by the cameras and shading screens. He was on duty, one hundred percent, and no casual observer would guess from his aloof appearance that the woman he was guarding had recently become his lover.

Except maybe Mateo.

He prowled the open air restaurant/bar under the pretext of making sure all was in readiness for the conventioneers arriving that evening. His once considered coup in bringing a group of international hotel chain bigwigs to his south-of-the-border resort for their annual conference seemed to have slipped a notch in his priorities as he watched Toni with a stormy glower.

She'd hurt his feelings. Beyond that, Toni feared she may have irreparably damaged their friendship. It had just been a kiss. But unlike any they'd exchanged before during their open and easy familiarity, this one meant something more than a fond gesture. When Mateo had leaned in to claim her lips the night before out on the glassy ocean, in his mind, he'd meant to lay claim to far more. Shocked to view him as a man instead of as her lifelong companion, Toni had overreacted.

His expression as she threw up her hands to shove him away had been one of disbelief, distress and ultimately betrayal.

What had he done to deserve such poor treatment? Suggest a solution to her troubles? Offer her an escape from the pressures that even now threatened to make her head explode? He'd reached out to her in concern and friendship asking her to consider a next step toward a partnership. Something she might have mulled over seriously until his head lowered. His features were obscured by darkness as he moved between her and the last of the setting sun.

She'd panicked. In that single moment, his faceless approach had become the embodiment of all her fears. And she'd reacted the way she always did when reminded of how it felt to be cornered and helpless. With a fierce, mindless resistance.

She knew she should apologize and try to recover what she still could of the feelings they had for one another. Feelings that went far beyond any shadow of intimacy she couldn't allow. She'd started toward him when his sister stepped in to engage him in somber discussion. Not wanting to interrupt when, as Veta's gaze cut to her then sharply away, Toni intuited that she was the topic of conversation, she turned back to the chaos Bryce was creating.

"We have to get these shots today, people. The ad firm needs them in New York by Friday. Antonia, dear, we need a miracle right now or this next campaign isn't going to happen and we're going to be out lots and lots of time and money."

He and the crew stood, staring impatiently at her, waiting for her to produce out of the clear Ixtapa sky the expected miracle.

And one was provided.

Zach looked up at her rapid approach, his calm facade tightening into consternation and alarm.

"Bryce needs your abs."

"I beg your pardon?"

"We need a great body to sex up a few swimsuit shots and yours is at the top of the list."

"I hardly think—"

"Yours is the only one on the list at the moment." Her voice lowered to an urgent pleading. "Be a good sport. I know you think my greatest vulnerability is out here in the open. Pose with me for a couple of pictures and I'll stay inside like a good girl for the rest of the day and won't give you any grief. Deal?"

"This isn't exactly the low profile I prefer to maintain when on the job."

"They'll think you're a random face in the crowd. Come on, Russell. Who's going to recognize you?"

"From the shoulders down only."

She breathed a sigh of relief. "Done." She turned to the increasingly agitated cameraman. "I've got your body double. Let's get to work."

Bryce pursed his lips. "Toni, I really don't think he's going to work."

Tired of arguing, Toni made her point by unbuttoning Zach's shirt. Bryce sucked a strangled breath and managed to say, "O—kay. Let's get this done. I need you and Mr. Atlas on the steps to the pool. Sit right there, Toni. Stud muffin, take off your loafers and wade right in behind her."

Seeing Zach's good sportsmanship beginning to wane, Toni caught his still healing hand and tugged gently. "Come on, stud. Get your feet wet."

Bryce posed them with Toni sitting on the curved steps and Zach standing behind her, his dockers soaked to the knees. With his hands fisted on his hips to hold his shirt open, the fierce disapproval in Zach's expression undocumented as Bryce took frame after frame.

"Toni, sweetie, I need some shots of how fabulous that suit looks on your tush. Stand up, doll, and get a handful of Mr. Muffin's yummy tummy."

Watching Zach's formidable jawline harden in granite, Toni buffed her palms playfully upon his belly with a charge of, "Lighten up, Russell. Where's your sense of humor?"

"You do realize," he began through gritted teeth, "that if he calls me that one more time, you're going to have to find yourself another cameraman."

Toni laughed, not at all intimidated by his gruffness. "Bryce talks to everyone like that. Even my father. Try picturing his expression the first time Bryce called him cupcake."

He must have been imagining it because his stance suddenly relaxed.

"Great. Marvelous," Bryce cooed. "Let's see a little more skin, hon."

"Which one of us is hon?"

Toni grinned. "I think that's you."

A scowl started to form. "If he thinks I'm going to drop my trousers…" He left that unfinished.

"I think he means your shirt."

And before Zach could stop her, Toni skinned it off, leaving his upper body…and the butt of his revolver exposed.

"Oh, that's a hot look," Bryce murmured, "but not quite right for our audience. Toni, be a good girl and cover that up along with any other inappropriate bulges."

Smirking at her tough bodyguard's distress, Toni slid in close, placing one hand to shield the pistol grip while the other slipped to the small of his back. Her chin rested just above belt level, her gaze lifted to his. The effect was startlingly sexy and unexpectedly intimate.

"Dynamite, Toni. Keep it coming. These ads are going to catch on fire. There's some great chemistry going on here. Up a little higher, Toni. That's it. One would almost think you two were in the middle of some hot, nasty affair. Let's hope that's what the consumer sees. Who wouldn't want to be having some fun in the sun with Mr. Muscles."

"I think we're about done here," Zach said under his breath, "before your voyeuristic friend has us boffing on the diving board for the sake of a few more consumer points."

Toni took a step back, stung by the harsh tone of his voice. She glanced around but didn't see Mateo. Wondering unhappily if he'd heard Bryce's unfortunate insinuation, she waved her hand in dismissal.

"Print them. I want a look before you send them out."

"Nice work, Toni. I think we've got some great stuff. Maybe Times Square quality. Buy your Greek god dinner on me."

Zach slogged out of the water, shrugging back into his shirt. At the moment, he seemed more Mercury, God of War, than the Adonis Bryce had captured on film.

"At least me mum won't know it's me up on some billboard in my skivvies," he was grumbling.

Picturing Zach Russell's flanks with a pair of damp white briefs hugging them to perfection forced Toni to turn and plunge into the pool. It took a dozen laps for the impression to fade to a manageable level. Zach was waiting with a hotel towel when she finally emerged.

"Remember, you promised not to give me any grief for

the rest of the day," Zach reminded as she wound the towel around her head instead of using it to cover her sleek water-glazed body.

Toni smiled. For the day perhaps. But that left the evening open.

Her unusual compliance should have made him immediately suspicious but Zach seemed too grateful to question her obliging mood.

After indulging in a massage, Toni returned to the room to order a tray of appetizers from room service that she shared with her roommate. While Zach prowled the room restlessly, she was content to go over the paperwork for the Aletta merge, opting graciously for the indoor table rather than the one out on the balcony. At two o'clock when the heat of the day was at its peak, she closed the patio doors, cranked the air conditioning and burrowed under the covers to enjoy a leisurely siesta nap. She slept soundly even as Zach continued to pace and wonder what she was up to.

She was just finishing her shower when Veta arrived with an envelope of photos from the morning's shoot. As Zach took the opportunity to take a turn in the bathroom, Toni spilled out the photos on the bedspread and plopped down to shuffle through them under Veta's watchful eye. Her own attention sharpened as she studied the pictures more closely.

She was used to Bryce's glossy renditions that cast her as some glamorous larger-than-life superwoman. But these pictures captured something different. Uncomfortable and wondering why, Toni went through them a second time.

"As Bryce would say hot, hot, hot."

Toni glanced up at Veta, a slight frown creasing her brow.

"Oh, come on, Toni, you've been infatuated with the man since you were eighteen. Genius that he is, Bryce just happened to catch that with his lens. A woman in lust will sell product. A woman in love confuses the issue."

"I'm not in love with Zach Russell."

But her protestations fell short when she looked at the pictures again. In them, the usually sharp, almost feral angles of her face seemed softened. Her uplifted gaze held something more akin to adoration than the expected adversarial gleam. At Zach's feet, the tiger had become a kitten.

"Good lord, we can't print these."

And she certainly couldn't let Zach or her father view them. She was seeing a woman with her heart laid bare and that was more vulnerability than she was willing to display to the general public.

"Bryce already sent them in. He figured you'd pull the plug and wanted to get another opinion from the ad execs. He thinks they'll ad a new dimension to our campaign, kind of a tough yet tender angle."

"At my expense," Toni groaned. "Who's going to take this moony-eyed female seriously in the business world?"

And how seriously would Zach take the worshipful glow in her eyes? She scooped the photos up and shoved them back into the envelope.

"Is Russell the reason you broke my brother's heart last night?"

Veta's calm, almost matter-of-fact comment blind-sided Toni, the same way Mateo's declaration had done. She leaned back against the headboard with a miserable sigh.

"Veta, you know how much Mateo means to me."

"But this near stranger, this employee fling of the moment, means more?"

"Russell has nothing to do with what I do or don't feel for Mateo. I just couldn't say yes to making a marriage into some kind of business deal."

"You know it's more than that. You know he cares for you, that he'd protect you and support you and be there for you. Will Russell give you those things? If you pay him, perhaps, but the minute his assignment is over, he's going to be gone, Toni. He's going to be gone and you'll be alone. For heaven's sake, girl, if you want to have a fling with the man, do it, but don't make it into something more than it's ever going to be. Don't confuse the moment with the rest-of-your-life. Russell is not a rest of your life kind of guy. Sex is not security."

"I know that."

But Veta didn't seem to hear her assertion. "You're a businesswoman. You know a good investment when you see one. Toni, when Premiero shows up tomorrow, you're going to want someone with you who'll take a stand next to you. You know what kind of man he is. He's machismo. He has no respect for your ability to run this company simply because you're a woman. But if you were to have a man there to deal with him, even if it's just for show, he'll pay attention."

That logic backfired. Toni's gaze narrowed. "I don't need a man to figurehead my ideas. I don't need a man to earn the respect I've worked for and I deserve."

Veta threw up her hands, familiar with where this argument was going. "Fine. Do it all on your own. Show your father you can wear the pants in the family. But remember what you're sacrificing."

"And what might that be?"

"Your safety, your happiness, love."

"But that sacrifice was good enough for you, Veta."

It was a cheap shot, but with Veta, there was no way to tell if the barbed comparison pierced the mark. She merely gave an icy smile.

"You and I are not the same, Antonia. You hide your fears in the shadows hoping they'll go away. I hunt mine down and take them out of the picture. You don't have the strength for the kind of future I've settled for. Premiero's going to eat you alive while your father sits back and enjoys watching the feast. Go ahead and do it on your own. But you'll regret it and you'll wish you'd made different choices."

"But they'll be my choices. I can live with that."

"Are they, Toni?" Veta's smile took on a mocking bend. "Can you really? Your past has made you a puppet to who's really pulling the strings. Consider who and what is making you dance before you tell me the choices are yours alone. You've been alone and you couldn't handle it. That's why Russell is here. You're using him to prop up your courage. What's going to happen when he leaves? When you have no one but yourself to rely on?"

"I have you," Toni answered quietly. "And Mateo. The three of us, like always."

Veta nodded, her haughty anger evaporating. "Like always. Remember that, Toni. Remember who you can count on."

And after Veta was gone, Toni sat in the silence with the envelope of photos hugged to her chest, her thoughts spinning.

Who was pulling her strings? Who was influencing the choices she thought were her own?

* * *

Something had happened.

Zach sensed it the moment he came out of the bathroom. To avoid any complications, he'd emerged fully dressed. Since the night before, he was cautious in his approach of his client. He'd think of her as his client. It was safer than thinking of her as his lover. That change in circumstance should never have transpired. The sad thing was, the really, really pathetic thing was, Zach didn't regret it. Not one heart-clenching, pulse-rocking moment of it.

The aftermath had been a minefield of dangerous emotions because he wasn't sure how Toni would react to their altered situation. He'd lain on the couch as if it was a bed of guilty nails, dreading what he'd do if she came to him, desiring it just as fiercely. But again, she'd shown a remarkable maturity by leaving well enough alone and they'd both had a chance to regroup their sensibilities in their solitary beds.

Then, there was the look she'd given him at the pool in front of the camera. That look was molten sex, burning through him as if their passions had come out of dormancy to detonate with atomic bomb force. For a moment all the blood had drained from his head to a lower, less predictable realm which left him swimming upstream against the lava flow.

However, when they'd returned to the room, she'd ignored him and left him chafing at that exclusion while, contrarily, he'd been craving her attention. He liked things simple and direct and his life had somehow gotten incredibly complex.

It was because of this woman who'd clung to his heart

as little more than a needy teen and now teethed upon it as a quixotic adult.

She was standing at the open slider, back just far enough to be out of sight from anyone who might be observing. Just as he'd taught her. She seemed engrossed in the fireball sinking in the west, setting the ocean afire with brilliant pools of orange and scarlet. Her pensive expression was as compelling as the repetitious surge of the tide, inviting him as a man to come to her side to slip a supportive arm about her and yet, at the same time, warning him away with hints that whatever plagued her thoughts was too personal to share. He stayed away, moving about the room making just enough noise for her to be aware of him if she chose to be. Still, he didn't anticipate her surprisingly calm question.

"Do you think someone is really trying to harm me or is it all some game?"

He paused to reflect for a moment, then gave her an honest response. "I think someone is intentionally abusing you mentally, but whether it goes beyond that to actual physical harm, I guess that depends on if they get what they want."

"What do they want?"

"It depends on what kind of crazy we're dealing with. Maybe it's someone trying to get close to a celebrity. Maybe it's one of your father's old business dealings carrying a grudge. Perhaps it's a competitor in the marketplace hoping to make you fail out of the blocks. Or maybe it's the one that got away, coming back to claim his due."

Toni shivered at that last suggestion. "And what do you think?"

"I can't afford to have an opinion without proof. I have

to be prepared for anything from the angry fashion critic to the enraged factory worker to the psycho who fantasizes about you wearing nothing but whipped cream."

"That's not an easy job."

"No. It's not." Especially not the whipped cream part.

"And I haven't made it particularly easy for you to do."

He smiled faintly at the understatement. "No, you haven't."

"Do you think things will get better or worse once Premiero gets here?"

"It depends on who's behind the threats and what they're trying to accomplish."

"So it's still game on."

"Exactly."

Her shoulders rose and fell upon a weary sigh. She nodded. "I'm glad you're here, Zach."

"For as long as you need me."

"And if I decide I need you forever?"

She turned toward him when he didn't answer right away. Her features were somber and closed tight against the sudden charm of his smile.

"You couldn't afford me, love."

"Because I'm too high maintenance?"

"No. Because I would be."

He watched her puzzle over that and before she could continue with the unsettling direction their conversation leaned toward, he interrupted with an unexpected suggestion.

"What say we take your sweetcakes cameraman up on his offer and dine al fresco on lobster and good wine at his expense until his pockets groan?"

Her response was guarded. "Really?"

"Pick a nice inconspicuous dress."

"In other words, go incognito."

"Just like any other normal couple."

He saw a speculative gleam flash in her gaze at the word *couple.* Or perhaps it was *normal.* Or worse, normal couple, as if they could come anywhere near approaching that definition.

Maybe for one night they could pull it off.

On this night, it was worth a try.

Chapter 12

Globes of light set into the raised brick planter beds cast a soft mood of romance over the outdoor patio. Candlelight flickered in hurricane lamps atop burgundy damask tablecloths, waking an answering gleam in the silver, crystal and bone china. The only music was the rhythmic percussion of the waves. Other than the server who issued them to their table and the bartender cleaning glasses beneath the thatch roofed bar, they were alone in the deepening twilight.

Antonia Castillo needed to learn something about concealment. A loose float of crinkly seafoam-green gauze with matching scarf covering her head and tinted glasses over her eyes didn't hide who she was any more than they could disguise her beauty. Her tanned arms and legs, bared and strong, magnificent bone structure as well as the confident way she moved, with chin high and haughty, betrayed her supposed secret identity to anyone who knew her or of her. She was a light beneath a basket, not quite a beacon, but no less the glow. Zach directed their host to a table near the wall overlooking the beach. That had the bar shielding them from a casual view from the hotel yet left them open to the cooling breeze coming off the water.

True to his plan, Zach ordered them lobster and charged it to Bryce's room. And with the gleam of the candle flame warming a reflection in the wine and in his eyes, he studied the woman across from him with a unswerving intensity.

"What?" Toni asked at last.

"This is nice, pretending to be regular tourists with nothing on their agenda but sipping local grapes and enjoying the sunset."

She smiled, wondering where he was going with the pleasant charade.

"If you were just a gorgeous face and I was some software salesman who'd won this vacation, what would we be doing this evening?"

"You mean if I didn't have someone out there trying to drive me crazy with their scare tactics and you weren't sitting here with a pistol in your Dockers ready to blast away at anyone who approached the table in order to collect your paycheck?"

His smile softened the hawkish lines of his face. "That's a bit cynical in interpretation but yeah. If we weren't those people."

"Well, we'd be trying to put a bigger dent in this bottle of wine. You'd be watching the sunset instead of over your shoulder for possible attackers. And I be thinking of ways to get you out of those Dockers as soon after dessert as it could be politely arranged."

His brows arched.

"Or," she continued, "we could settle for a walk along the beach."

"I'm not sure which would be safer."

"I'm guessing we'll be walking."

Her smirk was so knowing, so certain, Zach wished he could have proven her wrong. But he knew which of the two would be more dangerous. At this moment, with the artificial light bronzing her features and the generous curve of her cleavage, guarding Toni as a possible target on the beach was much safer than fending off Toni, and his desire for her, behind closed doors upstairs.

They sat watching the subtle change in the waters from blues to olive to silver grey and finally black. Lights winked on like fireflies on the surrounding hillsides and in the endless canopy overhead. Maybe it was the wine, maybe the beckoning curl of the waves. Toni couldn't remember such a moment of complete peace. She knew, of course, that she was simply crossing a valley on her journey from one difficult peak in her life to another but for now, she chose to linger in that contented lull, to experience that ordinary life fate and family had denied her.

She finished the last bite of her crusty cheese roll and washed it down with the remainder of her wine. Her attention drifted from the restless waters to the calm surface Zach Russell presented. Though he looked as relaxed as she felt, his gaze moved continuously in a pattern not unlike that of the cyclic waves. And that steady dependability drew her with equal fascination.

Veta had said he'd be gone as soon as the paycheck was cashed. Zach had never led her to believe otherwise. For as long as you need me, he'd said. Her reply to that hadn't

been an exaggeration. That need could easily extend to forever. When would she not need the grounding influence
his presence brought into her life? The sense of safety, of
stability, and just recently, of potential passion. Those
weren't things she'd willingly surrender even after the
momentary threat passed her by. Mateo had offered the
same benefits, the security and the support, but with him,
with her old, dear friend, there were none of the emotional
entanglements to add spice and excitement to the mix. It
was the tension, the challenge that Russell presented, as
well as the steadfastness that appealed to her.

What would it take to convince Zach Russell to stay?
Once the danger was past, she couldn't envision him as
content to follow her to her business meetings and stand
guard while she approved ad copy. Though he presented
a picture of outward stillness, he was a man of action and
movement. She recognized a kindred restlessness in him
because it drove her as well. Neither of them was made
for a sedentary existence.

Something pushed Zach Russell, something she didn't
understand. He was well educated with a wealth of diverse
interests. He appreciated fine things and creature comforts
yet chose a life of uncertainty and self-deprivation. Why
would a man choose to be nomadic, to court danger on be-
half of someone he didn't know, with no chance of gain-
ing notoriety or achievement. In his line of work, one
didn't win medals. There hadn't been much she could
learn about Russell's occupation other than it required
him to sleep with a passport and a pistol, to be ready at a
moment's notice to defend what exactly, she couldn't find
out. This week, he was defending her peace of mind. She
was sure that mission wasn't his usual high priority assign-

ment. A threatened athletic wear company CEO didn't exactly equate to maintaining world stability.

So why was he here, with her? Obviously, the international scene hadn't decided to take a break from chaos just to give him some free time on his hands. Was it for his friend Chaney, as he'd claimed, or was it something else, something more akin to a debt owed to an emotionally and physically broken eighteen-year-old who'd slipped through his protective net?

Was he here because he felt guilty about what had happened to her on his watch? Did he still view her as that unfortunate, damaged creature begging him for his silence?

That wasn't the impression she wanted him to carry when he left her side for his next assignment.

"Let's walk."

With shoes in hand, they trudged through the well-churned beach sand to the hard-packed strip washed clean by the waves. They followed another couple's footsteps until the next rush of water scoured away all evidence of their passing. Toni watched the water retreat, thinking how simple her life could become if only the past could be erased with such ease.

The next whoosh of the tide boiled in with a surprising amount of force. The surf sucked the sand out from under their feet even as the last roll of the wave foamed over them. Losing her balance, Toni grabbed for Zach's arm then continued to let her fingertips find refuge in the bend of his elbow. This close to the water, the sound of the swells coming in was like a roar. She had to speak loudly to be heard over it.

"What will you do next?"

"Next?"

"After you're finished here."

He was silent for a long minute. The pause grew uncomfortable.

"Afraid if you tell me, you'll have to kill me?" Her
laugh sounded strained even to her ears.

"I try not to look beyond the job. But I'm sure I won't
be without work for long. This is the closest thing to a vacation I've had since completing my agency training, so
I'm in no particular hurry to get back to it."

The job. Toni swallowed down the harsh reality of that
statement. That's what she was to him. A job nicely set in
paradise. What wasn't to enjoy? Throw in a little fling on
the side as a bonus and what complaints could he possibly
have?

Or was it that simple? Nothing about Russell was simple.

"Don't you ever get tired of it? Of the traveling and the
danger?"

"Every time I unpack my bag."

"And where is that?"

"France."

He didn't seem to want to get more specific than that
so she let it go for the moment.

"Do you think about retiring?"

"Every time I unpack my bag." She could see his faint
smile in the fading light. His was a strong profile, all clean,
bold, honest angles. Only the diamond stud winking in his
ear showed a bit of the flamboyance usually concealed by
the job.

"So what keeps you going? No good retirement plan?"

He chuckled but wouldn't be baited into revealing more
than a vague sketch of his life. "Unfinished business."

"Personal or professional?"

"You certainly ask a lot of questions." A touchy subject. She could read his reluctance and discomfort in the sudden tightening of his jawline.

"I like a good mystery and you, like it or not, are one big question mark."

"I'm really a very simple fellow."

Now she laughed. "Right. I'm sure it says that on your four-volume passport right under your license to kill."

"Let's start back."

What she really wanted to do was continue going forward. She knew nothing about Zach Russell and he didn't seem inclined to give her any additional insight. She was sure he had a dossier on her that gave away every secret from her grade school transcripts to the locations of her moles and scars. And he knew things not contained in any file. It wasn't fair that he should be a blank page. It made him all the more transient as he passed through her life again.

"So what will you do when you hang up your gun?"

"Like one of your American gunfighters?"

"Something like that."

"I hadn't given it much thought."

She snorted. "You give everything way too much thought. I can't believe something as unavoidable as your future wouldn't warrant some consideration."

"Not everyone in my profession has the luxury of a future."

She hadn't thought of that, of the daily danger of what he did. She was sure there was some percentage in a chart somewhere telling what his chances were of actually making it to the Golden Years. But she wasn't sure she wanted to hear it. She fell silent, her mood sinking into somber realms.

"A restaurant."

His sudden claim startled her from the morose turn of her thoughts. "What?"

"My retirement plan. I'd like to open a place of my own, nothing fancy or extravagant but with a regular clientele you could join for a glass of wine at the end of the day. Some place along the Mediterranean maybe, where life moves a little slower and the finer things are appreciated."

"Haven't given it much thought, eh?"

Funny thing was, she could picture him there, surrounded by the pleasing scents of olive oil and simmering sauces and an enviable wine cellar. He'd spend his mornings inventorying ingredients for the evening's specials. Instead of poring over intelligence files, he'd be researching old family recipes. He'd trade hunkering down in the shadows of some covert foreign conflict for swapping stories about past adventures over a checkered tablecloth and crusty bread. His future dream would also feature family of his own, children underfoot and an indulgent wife keeping the home fires simmering in the background. It was a nice picture, a pretty postcard existence a world away from her own.

What would her own future hold? A boardroom. An office in a lakefront skyrise. Work that consumed her days then went home with her every night, becoming her constant companion in lieu of a significant other. A life like the one her father led all alone at the top of his empire. With no one to share the successes, big or small.

A bleak forecast.

They left the water's edge to cross the sandy beach.

Music was playing from somewhere in a soft accompaniment to the continual rumble of the waves. Zach had already returned to ready mode, his gaze scanning for potential problems. Toni could have told him the greatest threat to her wasn't in the bushes. It was insidiously stalking inside her. The fear, the isolation, the insecurity. Those were the things endangering her future, distracting her from what needed to be done, from what should have been seen. She needed to clear her mind of those old cobwebs from the past so she could turn with sharpened attention to who was trying to destroy her. She needed to get focused, to be stronger, taking control of the destiny someone wanted to deny her. So far they'd used weapons that attacked her weaknesses to tear down her confidence and make her doubt her own decisions. But in doing so, they'd unintentionally brought to her the only means of defeating their scheme. Only one source could fortify her sense of self and drive away the loneliness that was her greatest enemy. And he was here beside her. Zach Russell was the cure for all that moved against her, for all who thought to turn her frailties into weapons to fatally wound her.

Now, if she could only find the courage to take the cure.

He tucked her hand into the sheltering bend of his arm. As they stepped into the glass elevator, her touch ceased being passive. At the slow stroke of her fingertips down his inner arm, Zach's attention jerked from surveillance to an alarmed inquiry as the doors slid shut behind them. As the elevator rose, Toni decided it was time to raise the stakes.

"You asked me what I'd do if we were different than who we are, but you never told me how you'd like this evening to end if we were a normal couple finishing up a romantic walk in the sunset."

"No, I didn't."

My, but he was cautious, unwilling to give anything away. She held the back of his hand in her palm while her fingertips traced inviting swirls up to the line of the brief bandaging he still wore. His gaze may have been guarded, his expression distant, but he made no attempt to pull his hand away. He could have stopped her with that simple gesture of objection, but he didn't.

"I told you that I'd be thinking of ways to get you out of your pants and into mine." She leaned closer, letting her body sway seductively until they were nearly touching. He'd gone totally still, yet she could imagine the frantic turnings in his mind. "Can you honestly tell me you haven't been wondering the same thing?"

"I've been busy thinking of ways to keep you safe."

She smiled at his stiff reply. "But I am safe. I've never felt more secure than when we were together last night."

A flicker of panic skirted his gaze. "That may have been a mistake."

"It didn't feel like a mistake. Are you telling me that you regret it happened?" She pressed into him, layering herself upon his body like a soft fitted sheet. He didn't answer her in words. His physical response spoke clearly enough. She reached down with her free hand to outline that impressive reply.

"Toni, don't complicate things," he warned quietly. Still, he hadn't moved or resisted her increasingly attentive touch.

"You like things simple and direct. Let me be direct. Tomorrow, it's back to business for both of us but tonight

I want that fairy-tale ending that comes after two normal people share dinner together and a walk on the beach in paradise. If that's not what you want, too, just say so."

His answer was to step back abruptly, severing the connection between them both physically and emotionally. He stared at the floor numbers lighting above the door, his concentration fierce, his jaw a block of stone.

Pride wouldn't let her pursue the matter further. She'd asked and he'd answered with a brutal clarity. She'd pretend it hadn't torn her heart in two.

When the doors parted, she started forward. Zach caught her arm, delaying her exit, she thought for security's sake. He pulled her back against him while the doors closed.

"That was our floor," she protested faintly, refusing to look around so he could see the anguish sparkling in her eyes.

"I wasn't ready to get off," was his soft reply.

She tried to turn then but his arms curved about her middle, binding her to him, holding her close but not tight. His mouth sketched a warm line from her temple to her left ear, exciting a hard shudder from her as his tongue traced along that delicate whorl. He continued down to suck suggestively at the side of her neck and nibble the sensitive curve to her shoulder as the elevator rose to the top and started down again.

"Push for our floor, love." His words whispered moist and hot against her skin. He was definitely pushing her buttons as he pressed the hard length of him against the groove of her buttocks. One of his hands slid low, cupping her firmly. She lit like a blow torch.

The distance from the elevator to the door of their room

was like a marathon. By the time he fitted the key, she was gasping for breath and fighting against the weakness trembling through her limbs. She collapsed against the inside of the door while he turned on a few strategic lights and did a quick yet thorough search of the premises. Then he came back to her, flattening her to the door panel with the full press of his body. Their mouths came together, all heat seeking hunger as impatient hands quickly rid one another of the barrier of clothing.

He lifted her, naked, from the pooling of her garments. He carried her to the bed then followed her down to the spread, covering her with his hard contours. And when she felt just the tiniest start of alarm, he quieted her panic and quashed her dark memories beneath an unhurried kiss.

And he made love to her, lavishing her with a healing touch, soothing raw remembrances with the slow stroke of his tongue, building strong new emotions that could conquer the first signs of panic with an anticipation of pleasures to come. He taught her the power of her own body's responses, how to ride the urgent crests of sensation and drift in languorous fulfillment on the tide of lingering contentment. And he made her feel secure enough to speak of the past that haunted her.

"He was so angry."

"Who was, love?"

"Steve Jenson. That was his name. Funny, I never think of him by name, only by what he did."

Zach came up on his elbow to regard her with a tender intensity. "Because the ransom wasn't paid?"

Toni stared straight up at the ceiling, her expression closed and inaccessible. "The entire time I was in that cold, nasty place, the only thing that kept me hanging on was the certainty that my father would rescue me and punish those responsible. I was sure of it. It was inconceivable that he wouldn't, that he would choose his money over my safety. Inconceivable." She fell quiet for a moment, reliving that sense of stunned surprise and ultimately, betrayal, even now. "I was so angry I wasn't even afraid at first. Not at first."

Can you believe he wouldn't pay a penny to save his own kid?

No, she couldn't. The shock of it had settled in so deep and so harsh that her captor's next fierce sentiment almost went unheard.

I guess I'm going to have to find another way to get paid.

Toni's eyes squeezed shut. His voice echoed in her memory, so fierce and furious, so ugly with the need to inflict pain. She began to tremble, as she'd trembled then, in fear, in anguish. Because rescue wasn't coming. Because hope was gone.

"He can't hurt you now."

Zach's firm summation wedged between the horror of those bleak, desperate days and the reality that she'd survived them. She'd survived them long enough for Zach Russell to find her. Long enough for Veta to put together the pieces linking the potting soil found in Toni's dank prison to the delivery driver from the plant nursery and to put an end to her attacker's life with a bullet to the head. But those two events never closed the circle of fear. Because the rest of the truth died with Steven Jenson.

Where's the money?

"They never found his accomplices." Toni spoke from out of the depths of her pain and panic, bringing to the forefront the anxiety that continued to stalk her peace of mind. "After we returned home, the case grew cold and was closed."

"And you kept all your secrets closed up inside you."

She glanced at him, her eyes shiny, reflecting the bleakness of her soul. "What choice did I have? I wanted it to be over. I couldn't go through it again. I couldn't drag my family name through it. The scandal would have followed me. I never would have been able to escape it."

"Have you? Escaped it? What good has carrying all that shame and fear for all these years all alone done?"

Her lips pinched together but she had no answer to seal inside. No reason that was good enough, except one. Zach could see it etched in the torment twisting her expression.

"He wouldn't pay for your release and you've been paying that price over and over ever since. It's not your debt, Toni. You did nothing wrong. Stop paying for it."

"But it is. It wouldn't have happened if I hadn't broken the rules. Your rules, Zach. I gave them the opportunity. I made it possible."

His reply was low and forceful. "It would have happened anyway. If not then, then another time. You think this whole thing just popped into Steve Jenson's head when he saw you unescorted outside that club? It had been planned, Toni. Everything was arranged except when."

"And I walked right into it."

"You were an eighteen-year-old girl. It wasn't your job to protect yourself. That was my job. And I failed you."

He failed her because it had been easier to break a young girl's heart than one of his precious rules. And he'd been paying the price for that ever since.

It was Toni who made the decision for both of them.

"We've paid enough, me for my pride, you for doing your duty. Maybe it's time we both let our secrets go. What do you think, Russell? Think we can move on without the weight of all that guilt?"

"I think it's worth a try. Let's move on, shall we?" He bent to kiss her.

Her answer sounded suspiciously like a sigh.

They both slept deep and dreamless in a tangle of one another's embrace. Daylight flooded the room when a single click woke Zach to a duty he'd almost forgotten.

Chapter 13

The sight of a naked Zach Russell throwing himself across Toni with gun in hand stopped Veta and Mateo Chavez in the doorway. Toni grabbed for concealing covers. A stunned silence fell over the four of them that was finally broken by Veta's stilted explanation.

"I knocked earlier when you didn't show up for this morning's meeting. When no one answered, I went to Mateo for a key. I thought something was wrong."

"As you can see, sis," Mateo concluded as shock gave way to an awful stiffness, "we are intruders, not rescuers. Forgive us."

He gripped his sister's arm and hauled her from the room. The sound of the door slamming sent home the enormity of what had just happened. She'd missed a meeting. She'd been discovered in bed with her bodyguard.

And seeing him braced in front of her, gloriously unclad, she had no desire to leave the tangle of covers.

But Zach had other ideas. He'd already shifted into professional mode, albeit a rather-tarnished-by-embarrassment professionalism. He was snatching up his clothes before Toni could make any other suggestion as to how to spend the morning. He didn't apologize. She didn't think she could have stood that. But his rigid lack of communication was almost worse. And in her uncertainty, all Toni's insecurities resurfaced behind a protective shield.

"Get showered," Zach ordered tersely. "You're not that late. Perhaps you haven't been missed."

What was missing was a little tender emotion from the man who had rocked her sensual world all night long.

"Are you afraid this lapse of judgment will cost you your job? That Veta's calling my father and you won't get paid?"

And in that moment, Toni realized that that's what she was afraid of, that her father would be called. That he would view her behavior as a sign she was incapable of taking over her mother's business.

But Russell was not now and had never been intimidated by Victor Castillo.

"I'm afraid our lapse of judgment will compromise my effectiveness in keeping you safe," was his curt reply. "Get dressed."

"We can't keep the world waiting, can we?"

She flung back the sheet and strode fiercely to the bathroom. As she stalked past him, Zach was tempted to reach out, to seize her in his arms, to pull her up against him and kiss the haughtiness from her expression because he could see the wounded vulnerability he caused huddling behind it.

But he let her walk by. He forfeited the moment that

would have healed the awkwardness between them to pre-
serve a sense of less complicated distance.

Because there was nothing simple about his response
to the sight of her all sleek, sleep tousled and in the buff,
as she closed the door on him.

Her staff was on their third cup of coffee and fighting
over the remaining pastries by the time Toni strode in clad
in an severe business suit and an equally aggressive mood.
As Zach took his inconspicuous place at the door, she accepted coffee and plunged into the meeting without apology. No one would guess how shaky that outer sheen of
confidence was.

She briefed those closest to her on the merger between
her family and Angel Premiero, laying out the anticipated
transfer of the company base to Mexico and a prospective
shift in job titles and obligations. The mood was somber
and the lack of optimism worried Toni as much as the speculative glances going between her and the silent sentinel
at the door. How many rumors had they heard concerning
Premiero? About her reason for being late to the meeting?
She couldn't afford to let their opinions matter. This was
the day she left the right to a personal life behind, the day
she became wedded to her mother's dream.

It wasn't as though she'd had any better offers.

They would celebrate the union of Aletta's international allure and Premiero's money at the Royale's highly
publicized hotel conference. Premiero had been sinking
funds into that arena as well, buying up foundering prop-
erties and transfusing them with the necessary capital to
update and compete. Toni would accompany him as his
guest to the formal event.

Premiero's yacht would moor at the marina in the early evening, allowing them time to exchange pleasantries and change into formal wear. Their meeting the next morning would be all business. She had all the figures, all the paperwork, all her father's instructions. What she didn't have was a good feeling about the whole venture. She'd studied the books. Despite her father's dire prophesies, she didn't see the same downward spiral in profits that precipitated the move and the new partner. Perhaps it was her inexperience, or maybe her reluctance to go cross grain of her mother's wishes. The merger sat uneasy, like a heavy meal, only this discomfort wasn't going away.

And her personal life wasn't settling any better than her professional one.

The meeting went on throughout the morning and into the early afternoon. Her mind should have been consumed with the changes they were about to undertake, but her traitorous thoughts kept drifting to the impassive guard at the door. She never looked his way, fearing her co-workers would make too much of it…or that Zach Russell would.

His actions of that morning confused her. He'd all but run from the bonding intimacies they'd shared at dinner, on the beach, in her bed. It would be one thing if she'd initiated a closeness he didn't appreciate. But he'd given her no sign that he didn't welcome every wonderful thing that had transpired from sand to sheets. Was it because he woke to the new day with a renewed dedication to his cause? Or did discovery by Veta and Mateo expose more of their relationship, as well as his attributes, than he was ready to have made public?

Either way, for whatever reason, he'd thrown the hated Rule Three back into the mix and her pride would not allow her to make any of the objections that teethed upon her heart.

The issue with Zach Russell would just have to wait until business with Aletta was concluded.

So how to deal with him until then?

Preoccupation seemed to work. She refused to let her attention be drawn from concern over the night's meeting with Premiero. She returned to the suite to take a brutally cold shower and change from tough executive to tougher prospective partner, opting for baggy cargo shorts and a black tank top instead of the respectful feminine attire that would appease Premiero's macho traditionalism. She didn't want him to think she was desperate to impress him or overly concerned with his opinions. She would approach him as an equal, as the new head of Aletta, as the daughter of his friend, as someone to be negotiated with, not bulldozed over. And for that to succeed, she couldn't be distracted by a certain British bodyguard.

He made it easy for her by remaining as far in the background as possible, by not addressing her, by becoming all but invisible. Yet her senses still thrummed with her awareness of him.

He rode in the front seat of the car, next to Tomas, giving her VIP status in the back. And on that big black leather seat, she'd never felt so alone.

The marina in Ixtapa bristled with the masts of elegant sailboats and stood hull to hull with sleek yachts. Its calm waters sheltered by a ring of mountains, it provided a parking lot for the rich at the doorway to the resort community. As the sun glazed the surrounding hills in reds and golds, Toni sipped a glass of wine from under the canopy of a water's-edge restaurant. Sinking daylight dazzled off the water and from the side of the ultramodern building that had meticulously muraled sides painted to reflect a mirror image of the harbor.

It was quiet, the lazy blanket of humidity settling in with the clouds atop the far range. On the nearby deck of one of the huge pleasure boats, a senior citizen in garish plaid shorts was polishing the gleaming rails while his toy poodle raced along the length of the craft yipping at something in the water.

At first, Toni thought it was the birds who swooped down to make quick work of the crusty bread bits she tossed for them that excited the little dog. Then she noticed a long irregular shape drifting on the languorous current. Garbage floating in this luxury playground? She didn't think so. Shading her eyes, she detected four distinct segments beginning with a small noblike protrusion, then a broad flat surface, another slightly mounded shape then a spiky ridge that lazily ruddered through the water to guide the object between the boats. The greedy birds scattered and the dog's barking intensified. It was then she realized what she was watching. A prehistoric predator serenely navigating the glassy surface as if it wasn't out of place amid the affectations of the rich.

"Premiero."

Toni frowned, thinking Zach's soft spoken remark referred to the bold crocodile as it drifted out of sight behind one of the moored seventy-four-footers. She glanced up to see a figure approaching down the dock, framed by the glare of the setting sun, and knew him instinctively. Another predator, not so different from his cold-blooded brethren hunting amongst the wealthy.

Angel Premiero was very much her father's peer. He had the same arrogant stride, wore the same expensive suits and had the same toothy smile that never lit the flat sheen of his dark eyes. A crocodile in Armani shoes.

"Antonia, how beautiful you are," he called in a voice that had yet to shed the heavy accent the way her father's had. "So grown up, yet I still see the mischievous child in the lovely woman you've become."

He boarded the floating dining platform, followed by four of his personal aides and the entire fawning staff of the establishment. He gave Russell a quick assessing notice as the bodyguard abandoned his seat for him. Then he was all icy charm as his attention turned back to Toni.

"So like your mother."

"Thank you, Señor Premiero."

"It used to be Uncle Angie," he chided, settling into the seat across from her.

"That was before I grew up."

His smile never faltered. "So like your mother." That didn't sound quite like a compliment. "Thank you for coming to meet me."

"It was the very least I could do for my father's oldest friend." The very least.

"And your new partner."

She dodged the issue by saying, "We have much to talk about."

They shared a glass of wine while she filled him in on her father's health and activities. She purposefully skirted any twists in the conversation that might lead toward business. There would be time for that tomorrow. Tonight, she wanted to get a sense of the man.

And it didn't take her long to dislike the feeling that set-

tled over her, the same one that had the little poodle barking wildly at a danger it didn't understand but recognized
intuitively.

Time didn't allow for much reminiscing and soon
Tomas was chauffeuring them back to the Royale for the
evening's meet and greet.

Toni dressed carefully, not as a CEO, but, for this evening, as a woman taking full advantage of that fact. She
told herself it was to impress Premiero, but another small
nagging voice whispered it was because she wanted to feel
the appreciative heat of Zach Russell's stare.

He remained distant and on duty even after they returned to the suite. By the time she emerged from the
bathroom, he was already sleekly clad in evening wear
with the diamond glinting roguishly in his earlobe. He
could pretend uninterest with his stance, but there was no
disguising the ravenous quality of his quick once-over
sweep.

The dress was a stunner, sophisticated, classically sexy.
The slinky black fabric poured down from spaghetti straps,
sliding over her curves like a lover's hands and accentu-
ating the length of her legs with the slenderizing sweep of
its floor-length cut. A sassy touch of jade green peeked
from the edging of the fluid neckline and flirted under-
neath the side-draped swag of fabric rippling down from
her left hip. A sheer black scarf looped about a neck dra-
matically bared by her glossy updo and the elegant spar-
kle of emerald stud earrings. Bold siren hues enhanced
lips, eyes and brows, giving her a forties screen star quality both glamorous and ultra feminine.

"Ready?" Zach managed at last, once he could pry his
tongue from the roof of his mouth.

"Willing and able," she concluded, offering her elbow.

The event was in full swing by the time Zach released her at the door. Part of her longed to stay at his side, protected by his nearness, emboldened by his presence. However, she didn't hesitate to stride into the mix, chin lifted with a conquering attitude as she zeroed in on Premiero.

He regarded her with a look she was well familiar with. It was very traditional, almost insultingly chauvinistic, that possessing, undressing look. The women-as-objects assessment her father gave to members of the opposite sex. A look meant to flatter but often had a different agenda, one that was demeaning and domineering. One her mother had never tolerated because, she'd told Toni at a young age, it made her feel less human, less equal. And she'd taught her only daughter never to accept less.

"Señor Premiero, good evening. Thank you for inviting me as your guest."

She extended her hand but instead of shaking it, he carried it in courtly fashion to his lips. His greying mustache was almost obscenely soft against her knuckles.

Toni withdrew her hand firmly, her smile razor-sharp. His, contrarily, was smug with the knowledge that he'd unsettled her. Then he studied her more closely.

"You didn't like my gift? It displeases me that you chose not to wear it."

Her fingertips went to her adornment-free throat. Her tone was as sharp as those bits of silver cutting into the base of her neck. "As it displeases me that it's part of an assault investigation."

"My aide told me there was an unfortunate incident." He made a tsking sound but his stare remained unmoved by the thought of her near tragedy.

"Unfortunate is a rather odd word to use regarding an attempt on my life."

"Had it been someone's intention to kill you, don't you believe they would have succeeded?"

She met his unblinking stare with an unwavering directness. "And what do you think the intention was?"

"In my country, it is almost always more beneficial to use intimidation. Murder is so…final."

"But an occasional occupational necessity, is that it?"

His smile spread like an oil leak. "Why, Antonia, what kind of business is it that you think I do?"

"A purely hypothetical question."

"Then, yes. I suppose it is an unfortunate solution to some problems."

"There's that word unfortunate again."

"What's the quote? Fortune favors the bold?"

Was he standing there bold as a brass band admitting that he'd orchestrated the attack on her at her father's home? Was he even going so far as to insinuate that the outcome could become deadly if she didn't capitulate?

She fought the sudden chill of dread tiptoeing across her bared skin. With her smile firmly in place, she cast a covert glance about the room, seeking the reassuring sight of Zach Russell. Russell would know what to make of Premiero's slick remarks.

But she found she wasn't the focus of her bodyguard's attention.

He was by the entry doors speaking to a woman whose back was to her. A sleek back nearly bared by the daring plunge of her silver evening gown. He was smiling at whatever she said and something in his expression seized Toni's heart in an anxious crush. The woman's hand rubbed the sleeve of his jacket in a blatantly familiar gesture, one he didn't attempt to evade.

And as Toni watched, her emotions knotting, a room key was passed from the elegant redhead to her usually stoic bodyguard.

The exchange was quick, discreet. Like a thin blade slipping between the ribs in search of a vital organ.

The woman left the party. Zach waited a moment, two, then approached Veta who was sipping a cocktail while entertaining the amorous intentions of some young executive with an amused glint in her eyes. As Zach spoke to her, her gaze flashed up to where Toni stood and she nodded. Toni recognized the signal. The ball had been passed. She was now in Veta's hands.

Freeing Russell to abandon his post, room key in hand, in pursuit of someone else.

"Darling, it's been far too long."

Zach returned the embrace, enduring the hurried kisses with a good-natured grin until she stood back to scrutinize him.

"You're too thin. You haven't been taking care of yourself."

"And look at you in that dress," he countered. "Are you out to snag me a new stepdad, Mum?"

She rapped him under the chin. "Cheeky boy. I've buried a husband and outlived two stepfathers. I think I've retired from the marriage business. I seem to be a bad investment."

"No man looking at you in that dress would think so."

"That's because men tend to think with the wrong organ, dear."

Zach laughed at his mother's typical straightforward-ness. But he hadn't lied. Cecilia Roberts at sixty-two was as fit and firm as a woman twenty years younger. It came from a life of constant motion. At work, at play and rarely at rest, she was a dynamo of enviable success. But the one thing she desired most continued to elude her. And Zach knew it would only be a matter of time before she re-minded him of it.

"I didn't know you were coming down for this, Mum. I would have met you at the airport."

"I only just decided when I found out you were here."

His eyes narrowed. "And how did you find out I was here?"

Her expression was blameless. "Jack told me."

"Good old Jack. And what else did he happen to let slip?"

"Don't be cross with Jack, darling. He is your best friend and has your best interests at heart."

"Really? And what has that to do with you being here?"

"You never used to be this suspicious," she scolded, avoiding the question.

"You never used to give me a reason. Give over, Mum. What mission are you on?"

"A purely selfish endeavor, I confess. I may have gone out of the marriage business, but that doesn't mean I'm any less interested in becoming a full-time grandmother." She turned toward the mirror over her dresser on the pretext of checking her flawless makeup. But it was to covertly gauge his reaction to her outrageous claim.

Zach groaned. Here it comes. "I'm not here looking for a bride, Mother." The formal address advised her that he was irritated and that she'd gone too far.

She was unimpressed.

"I know you're not looking. Because she's here."

He stood, mind boggled by her deductive stretch of logic. "Who?"

"That girl, the one you risked your career for. The one that's made you fierce and rather unpleasant for the last ten years. She's the reason you're here and the reason I've come to talk to you since you can't seem to find the time to visit me for chat."

He felt the required guilt over her last statement, but that made him no less prickly about her interference—and Chaney's—in his personal affairs.

"I am here on a job. Don't read more into it than that."

"Dear, a blind man could read more into it than that. And no, Jack didn't have to tell me anything. I could see it in your eyes after it happened. You made yourself responsible because of what you allowed yourself to feel for her. Is that why you're here, Zachary? Because you think you owe her something? Or is it because of something you think you might owe yourself? Like a chance at what your father and I had."

He shut down all emotion, all expression but it was too late to disavow a truth she already seemed to know.

"It's a job, Mum. There's nothing more in it for me. There never will be."

"Because you're not finished punishing me yet?"

Her remark hit like a rabbit punch. "Whatever do you mean by that?" He could see by the way her eyes welled up in long unspoken misery that this went far beyond the nonexistent grandchildren.

"If your father hadn't been in such a hurry to meet me, he wouldn't have been so careless. And he would still be alive. And you blame me for that. And him."

"I never said that."

"No. You never said anything in words. You let your actions speak for you. In the way you live your life by such strict, unbending guidelines, by shutting yourself off from anything that could distract you from your duty. By the way you wear the diamond from your father's ring and continue his causes like some holy crusade. And because he failed to keep himself safe, you're possessed with this need to protect the rest of the world from similar folly, starting with yourself."

He didn't respond. He couldn't. He could only stand, frozen in place, listening to her dice his noble ambitions into inconsequential pieces.

"But something in this girl made you think about more than duty. She made you glance off that path of self-righteousness for just one moment and in that moment, the inconceivable happened. And now you think you're to blame for whatever she suffered because you took a moment to consider a different road. That's bunk, Zachary, sheer nonsense, and I cannot believe I've allowed you to get away with wallowing in such unbecoming self-pity for so long."

"Is that what I'm doing?"

The frigid civility in his tone warned her to tread carefully should she decide to continue in the reckless direction she'd chosen. She gentled her approach but refused to relent.

"And you're doing it badly. You were in love with this girl and you figured with typical male arrogance that if you repaid your debt of guilt, you'd be free of those feelings. I can tell by your bad manners that you've found that not to be the case. Am I right?"

"What if it's not? What if I do have feelings for her and

because I'm so busy mooning over her, someone slips past me and snuffles out her life? I won't take that risk. I won't pay that price."

"It can't be the job and the job alone for the rest of your life. You can't make up for your father's momentary lack of caution or for your own brief human failing by living up to some impossible standard that will deny you any chance of happiness."

"Maybe I'm willing to forgo that happiness for the sake of seeing her safe from harm."

She considered that for a long moment then said, "Is she willing to do the same? Is it fair of you not to ask her that question before you go making all the decisions for your future without her?"

When he wouldn't respond, she sighed heavily but not in surrender. "How long are you going to stay angry with us?"

"I'm not."

"You're so angry you can't even admit the truth to yourself. And because you can't express that anger to him and, thank heavens you're too respectful to take it out on me, you have to vent it on any perceived evil the world puts in your way. When will it be enough to satisfy you? When will you stop punishing all of us for not following your rigid rules?"

"He didn't have to die, Mum."

Because his eyes glistened, she put a tender hand to his cheek. "I know. But he did. And you can't change that. You can't change what happened to Antonia Castillo. And you can't continue to blame him and yourself. What good is having a life if you're not allowed to live it? Think about that before you shut yourself up behind your duty and your rules. Think about how she'd prefer to spend her future. As a prisoner or a participant? Which do you think she'd pick? If she's the kind of woman you could love, I think I know the answer. Her safety won't always be your job, but her happiness could be. Think about it, darling. And think about one more thing."

He smiled faintly, wondering what she could rub into the wounds about his heart. "What's that, Mum?"

"I know Mateo Chavez has a past with your young lady."

Zach didn't protest her wording. It would have taken too much effort to convince her that Toni was not his young lady, nor would she ever be. "Your point being?"

"I've heard rumors, so I checked them out. It seems he's in desperate debt and is looking for a way out of his troubles."

"I've heard that, as well. To that thug Premiero?"

She placed her hand on his arm, squeezing gently. Warning him to brace himself. He did so by cautious increments.

"No, darling. To Victor Castillo. Be careful lest your enemy be someone closer than you think."

Chapter 14

It took Toni all of an hour to realize that she disliked Angel Premiero as much, if not more, than she distrusted his vision for Aletta.

Displayed at his side like a pretty object to be admired, she observed the way he worked the room and those in it. He was charming, then he was forceful, then, if that didn't subdue his opponent, he played the intimidation card. He was very good and placed it down with the skill of a cold professional. And he enjoyed watching the other person squirm.

He was making a point, of course. If she didn't toe the line he'd drawn for these others for her benefit, she would be on the receiving end of his calculating wrath. And she was sure it was terrible. Her mother had loathed her husband's childhood friend. Though she never said so, Premiero was the reason she would never agree to travel as a family to Mexico, where they'd be on Premiero's turf. And now Toni was beginning to believe Mercedes Castillo would want no different in regards to her company. Premiero was like a big cold-blooded jungle snake. Once he had a victim in the first loose coil, they were wrapped up and squeezed into submission before they knew they were in danger.

Toni understood danger. She could scent fear in the nervous perspiration he inspired in others as he leaned in too close and smiled too widely. He was a bully but, unlike her father, he lacked patience and finesse. The charm extended only so far before annoyance would give way to backstreet strong-arm tactics. That was the purpose of the foursome who followed him in a pack wearing expensive suits that purposely didn't conceal the fact that they were heavily armed persuaders to Premiero's way of thinking.

When he had finished pressing concessions from all who offered him some advantage in the hotel management field, he turned his attention to the next matter on his agenda. His smile sent a shiver to Toni's soul.

"So, Antonia, when shall we get the preliminary paperwork signed? How would tomorrow morning at ten work for you?"

"I'm not sure it's going to work for me at all, Señor Premiero."

"Angie, remember."

"Señor Premiero, I'm afraid I'm not ready to sign anything. After studying the books and projections, I think I'd like to commission another feasibility study."

"Your father has already done all that. All that's left for you to do is sign. Tomorrow at ten."

"I won't be signing anything tomorrow. In fact, I don't

think I'll be signing anything at any foreseeable time in the future." Time to put it plain. "I don't think you're what Aletta needs."

His features darkened, growing florid as fury pumped through him. "I don't think you understand. Your father has already put this deal in motion. Money has been invested as well as his word. You will carry out his wishes."

"I think it's you who doesn't understand, *señor.* My father's wishes no longer control the company. I do and I don't wish to do business with you."

She considered herself safe in the center of the glitzy crowd of moguls and managers. But she underestimated the volcanic heat of Premiero's blood once it was up. He caught her arm. His fingers pinched tight, creating the beginnings of distinctive bruises. Unmindful of who might notice, he stepped in, so close his aftershave stung her nose and she could see the red spider veins of dissipation in the whites of his eyes.

"Who do you think you are talking to, little girl? You have no place in an arrangement between men. Call Victor. He will talk sense into you. He'll tell you how much more is riding on this merger than just gym shoes and jog bras. It involves a debt long unpaid, one that will not be forgiven lightly should you decide to continue this foolishness. You have no power here. You are no more than big breasts in a skimpy shirt. A marketing tool to be exploited just as your father has done. Don't presume to be more than that. You are very, very mistaken if you think you'll be allowed to back out now. And very wrong if you think I would hesitate to prove it to you."

"Prove you're a smart man and take your hand off her." Russell's quiet command rumbled in like a sudden summer storm, all sizzle and crackling ozone against a deceptive black velvet sky. At his abrupt intrusion, Premiero's men jolted to a bristling attention as the potential for violence escalated times four.

"Tell them to heel. We're all gentlemen here and it would be rude to create a scene."

Premiero jerked a nod toward his men and they reluctantly stood down. For a long beat, he and Zach locked stares like two hungry beasts with a tender morsel trapped between them.

"Excuse me," intruded a feminine voice. "Mr. Premiero, might I have a word with you about a property in Puerto Vallarta? If I'm not interrupting anything."

Premiero's charming facade slid back into place as he regarded the elegant woman who'd approached them. "Señora Roberts, I always have time for you. My conversation here was finished." His glare touched upon Zach and Toni for a brief, furious instant to remind them that all was not settled, before he crooked an elbow toward the sleek and sophisticated Cecilia Roberts.

As they walked away, Toni recognized the daring back of the older woman's silver gown. She was the one who'd slipped Zach her room key. And now she'd appeared at a fortuitous moment to temporarily remove the threat of Angel Premiero. Coincidence? She glanced at Zach, a brow raised in question, but before she could demand the woman's identity, Veta and Mateo wound their way through the crowded room to join them.

"Have I missed something?" Veta asked, her narrowed gaze on the way Toni was rubbing her forearm.

"Mateo, could I have the use of a quiet conference room with a phone, an Internet link and a fax?"

"You can have one of the business offices."

"You can bill—"

He waved his hand, dismissing the suggestion. "Do not worry. I'll have coffee delivered."

"Thank you." Aware that they'd never had the opportunity to discuss what he'd walked in on that morning, she reached out a placating hand to touch his sleeve. "Mateo…"

His smile was thin and weary. "I'll arrange for the room and your privacy." He nodded stiffly to Zach and wasted no time in escaping them.

"Well?" Veta posed impatiently, looking between Toni and Zach. "What did I miss?"

"Prepare to batten down the hatches," Toni told her somberly. "I'm pulling the plug on the Mexico move."

"Premiero and your father aren't going to be happy."

Toni smiled grimly at that prophecy. "I'll have to get used to their disappointment."

Remaining in the background, Zach watched Toni kick back her second strawberry margarita. She'd had the darkened lobby bar area to herself for the past half hour and seemed content with her solitude. The enormity of her actions weighed in the sober lines of her face and in the slump of her shoulders. He could tell she was wondering if she'd done the right thing, for the company, for herself. He thought so. He thought she'd behaved honorably and with incredible bravery. And he would have told her so if her expression hadn't warned him away.

She'd made a dozen overseas phone calls from the small second-floor office, circling her wagons as she contacted Aletta's legal department, the head accountant, the marketing director and the head of the workers' union among others. Her demeanor was serious and decisive, and though she hadn't allowed him inside the room while she made the calls, he could read professional all over her. She was going to be great at her job, much more than boobs in a thin shirt, Premiero was going to be surprised to discover. He'd figure that out when he realized Toni had effectively stopped the merger cold.

He was going to be livid. And Zach would have to be prepared should his anger transform into an unpleasant retribution.

It was well past midnight. The conference mixer was still going strong up on the third floor. Occasional bouts of laughter and music drifted down through the open atrium. Hunched over the empty bowl of her glass, the flickering of the candle centerpiece etching a melancholy portrait as she stared sightlessly into space, Toni was the embodiment of it being lonely at the top.

"She needs you."

Zach started at the soft summation. He glanced at his mother, then back to the solitary figure. "She doesn't need anyone right now."

"You're wrong, Zachary. This is exactly when a woman needs to feel the support of those who care for her." She waited for her son to accept that role but when he remained silent, she shook her head sadly. "What a mother won't do to get grandchildren."

She headed for the lone occupant, ignoring the objecting sound Zach made.

"Mind if I join you?"

Toni looked up, puzzled to see the attractive older woman who'd come to her rescue earlier. "I'm not very good company, I'm afraid."

"I'll be the judge of that. You should be celebrating. It's not every day a lowly female gets the better of someone like Premiero."

Toni's brow furrowed. She studied the woman's name badge. Cecilia Roberts. The name meant nothing to her. "Do we know one another?"

"We have a mutual friend." She glanced back to where Zach was standing at his post.

"Oh. I see."

Cecilia chuckled warmly. "I don't think you do, dear. My name was Russell before it became Holmes then Roberts." At Toni's blank look, she concluded, "Zachary is my son."

"Oh." And finally she did see. The resemblance, the accent, the obvious affection between mother and son. "That was good of you to step in with Premiero."

She gave a derisive snort. "A pleasure. I loathe men of that ilk. I've come up against their brick walls my entire professional life. Neanderthals, the lot of them."

Suddenly it clicked. "There's no place like Holmes."

Cecilia laughed. "That was Archie's favorite ad campaign. Mine was Holmes is where the heart is."

"Home in on Holmes Inns. You're Archibald Holmes's widow."

"Rest his soul. I've never decided whether to bless him or curse him for leaving such an expansive hotel dynasty for me to run by myself. He had no family. I always hoped that my son might show an interest in stepping in so I could enjoy…other interests, but he has too much of his father's wanderlust and call to duty to settle behind the safety of a desk. Charles was a British diplomat. Zachary was raised in some of the most exotic and unsavory places on the planet. And dangerous. His father was killed in a car bombing when Zach was away at school."

Toni's heart twisted in a familiar ache. "My mother died in an auto accident when I was a teen."

Cecilia pressed a soft palm over her hand. "I met your mother at a Women in Business seminar in Atlanta. I was very impressed by her drive and intelligence. I was saddened to hear of her passing."

"She left me her company. Now I just have to make sure I live up to her trust in me."

Cecilia sighed. "Why do our children always assume that they bear the burden of our expectations? All a parent wants is for a son or daughter to be happy and to live well. All the other pressures they pull onto their own shoulders until they stagger under the weight of them. The way my son does."

Cecilia fell silent and though Toni was anxious to hear what she would say, she didn't press for an answer until the older woman was ready to give it.

"There had been death threats made against my husband. He was under heavy protection, under guard round the clock. He was coming home to England for our anniversary and to see Zachary compete in a diving competition. He refused to take us out of the country with him once the threats began. He was late getting out of a meeting and he had a plane to catch. He was in a hurry and decided not to take the extra time to have his vehicle checked before he got in. It exploded, you see."

Toni gripped her hand to convey her empathy and horror.

"Zach withdrew from the university and joined MI6. It was his belief that carelessness took his father's life, that if his body men had forced him to wait, that if he hadn't been so distracted by his desire to see us, he would have taken the necessary precautions that would have saved him."

"But he didn't follow the rules," Toni concluded quietly, awfully.

"And my son has been playing by them ever since. He's become a prisoner of them. He doesn't understand that those rules can be bent without being broken."

No, Toni realized. Zach wouldn't understand that. All he knew was that when the rules weren't followed, he suffered for it. With the loss of his father, with her abduction. Failures he felt responsible for whether logic applied to his reasoning or not.

What exactly was Cecilia Roberts expecting her to do about it?

The television over the bar had been playing a Spanish dubbed rerun of the Simpsons. Suddenly, the feed crackled and went to snow. Then another image flickered up in its place. The sound of a young woman's weeping drew Toni's attention and then she couldn't look away.

The bruised and bloodied young woman, her mouth and eyes taped shut, her hands and feet bound, cowered against a rough rock wall in a dimly lit root cellar. Crude camera work zoomed in to exploit the fear in her huddled posture as she snuffled behind the thick tape and shrank from the unseen threat hovering over her. She wore a stained electric-blue pullover top. A hand reached into the frame, seizing the garment by the neckline, pulling hard as the woman struggled wildly to free herself. Seams ripped as the girl jerked away and wriggled until she was left to shiver in her lacy bra.

"Darling, are you all right? Are you ill?"

Toni heard the concern in Cecilia's question, but she couldn't respond to it. Her head was filled with the terrified whimperings of the girl on the screen. A terrible cold seeped through her skin to her very bones. The taste of the young woman's fright filled her nose and mouth with a bitter bite of helplessness. She couldn't seem to draw a breath.

"Zachary, something's wrong."

Zach vaulted over the planter box separating the bar from the lobby area and came quickly to crouch at Toni's side.

"Toni, what is it?"

When she didn't respond, he followed her fixed stare to the television screen.

Where an eighteen-year-old Antonia Castillo wept in fear of her life.

Chapter 15

Acting quickly, Zach gripped the sides of Toni's chair and physically turned it so she was facing away from the awful image on the screen. To his mother, he said a curt, "Stay with her," then he was up, racing toward the bar.

The single employee was in the back folding freshly laundered bar towels. He looked up in alarm, expecting a stickup at least from Zach's forceful approach.

"Where does the signal for the television come from?"

The bartender, deciding he wasn't about to be robbed, pointed an unsteady finger. "From upstairs. In the main offices."

Zach was gone before the man could finish. He raced through the bar area where his mother had wrapped a pale and shaken Toni into a snug embrace, and charged up the stairs that bridged the lobby's central waterfall fountain. The majority of the upstairs offices were dark, the doors listing the names of various travel agencies locked for the night. One light shone at the end of the hall. The owner's office.

Mateo Chavez was seated at his empty desk working his way through a bottle of tequila. He'd been working hard from the looks of his sloppily loosened tie and even sloppier position in the chair. He blinked blearily at Zach, not bothering to hide his resentment.

"Are you alone up here?"

Zach's brusque tone must have cut through his stupor, for he struggled to sit up and focus. "Yes, I believe so. I was going to work on some accounts…" His voice trailed off as Zach disappeared in the adjoining rooms and he waited, perplexed, until the other man returned with a videotape carefully held by its corner by a tissue.

"Explain this."

"It's a tape," was all Mateo could offer, then he flushed and blustered. "I don't allow pornography here. I don't know who brought it, but when I find out, they'll be fired on the spot."

"It's not porn."

Mateo sagged back in his chair, trying to make sense of Zach's massive anger. "What, then?"

"It's a copy of the video Toni's kidnappers sent to her father when they demanded ransom. It was playing on the bar TV downstairs."

He blanched. "And Antonia?"

"Saw it."

"*Madre mio.* Who would do such a thing? And why?"

"That's what I mean to find out. How long have you been up here?"

"I don't know. Maybe a half hour."

"Have you seen anyone else?"

"No one. They are all tending the party. I was not in a festive mood so I came here to sulk, I guess you could say." His smile was self-deprecating.

"Who would have access to the tape player?"

Mateo shrugged helplessly. "Anyone on staff who knew how to program a VCR and use a remote. They could have started the tape from anywhere close by or just set the timer. We use it to show bootlegged American sports events." His voice softened. "Is Antonia all right?"

"No."

And with that, Zach left the office. There was nothing more he could learn there. The scene was open to anyone. The suspects were limitless. The chance of any finger-prints was incredibly slim, but he handled the tape with care out of habit. He wasn't a detective. It wasn't his job to follow up on criminal leads. His job was the fragile woman in the sports bar slowly unraveling at the seams.

"How's she doing?"

His mother looked up from where Toni was still hud-dled in her embrace. Her expression mirrored her concern. "She's in shock. Maybe we should call a doctor."

"No." Toni spoke up immediately, the word faint but no less firm. Zach understood. No publicity.

"I'll take her upstairs. Thanks, Mum. Get back to your party."

Cecilia surrendered the trembling figure with reluc-tance. "I'll discreetly ask about and see if anyone slipped away. Perhaps our friend, Premiero."

"Low profile, Mum."

"You needn't tell me that. Take care of your young lady. I'll take care of this old one."

While Cecilia headed for the stairs and her contemporaries, Zach lifted a limp and unprotesting Toni to her feet. With his arm about her waist and her head lolling upon his shoulder, a casual observer would think he was assisting a party-goer who'd had too much to drink. Her lack of responsiveness worried him, making him wonder if perhaps he should overrule her request and call in a physician.

He'd listened to her plea ten years ago. It hadn't been the right decision then, so why would it be now? He'd give her a little time to come around on her own. Just a little.

As they rode up in the elevator, Toni began to stir. She gathered her wits about her in gradual degrees, her posture strengthening, her breathing deepening, until he felt her push against him for release. He refused to comply. She wasn't going anywhere. His arms locked her more tightly into his side. She didn't struggle. Nor did she succumb to the closeness. She simply stood stiff and still until they reached their floor. When the doors opened, she moved beside him in a rigid autopilot, not speaking, not reacting, just following his lead.

She headed straight for the bathroom and in seconds, he heard the shower running. He took advantage of her absence to pop the video into the in-room VCR. Though every fiber of his being rebelled against it, he had to watch the tape all the way through in case it contained some clue to her abduction. Something they'd missed. Anything.

He'd watched the original ransom clip. Short and visceral in impact, it showed a terrified young woman, cut off from light, from safety, from contact with hope. But the entire, unedited tape went beyond mere intimidation, beyond isolation. It encapsulated the horror, graphically, aw-

fully, that Antonia had suffered at the hands of her ab-
ductor.

The monster had put it on film.

The water was so hot, it reddened her skin but Toni
couldn't feel the warmth. She leaned into the scorching
spray and scrubbed at a stain she could never remove. The
stain of shame, of guilt, of pain and fear. No amount of
cleansing could rinse away that inner blemish.

When her flesh stung and her knees were trembling, she
simply stood under the punishing pulse of the water and
let it beat down upon her bowed form. The sobs started
from a point deep inside her, from the hidden recess where
she'd locked away her sorrow and sense of blame because
it was too enormous, too horrible to confront alone. Most
of the time, she managed to keep it there, ruthlessly
cramped into that cold niche in her soul, where childhood
nightmares still roamed seeking a vulnerable moment in
which to escape.

This nightmare had refused to go tamely, to rest quietly. It roared to life at unpredictable intervals, shaking her
confidence, crushing her sense of self-worth, humbling
and reducing her to the lowest, most fragile state a
woman's spirit could know. Usually, she fought it, battling
to stuff the feelings, the remembrances, the sensations
back into that corner of her being where she could pretend
it was under control. But tonight she let the beast burst
free, let it ravage and howl while she sagged against the
slick, unsupportive tiles and weep as if her heart was
breaking.

She knew Zach was watching the tape. She knew what
he'd be seeing.

Smile for the camera, sweet thing. This is one show your daddy will never forget. I'm going to make you a star.

She sank down to her knees, her shoulders quaking, her arms wrapped about herself to provide a protection she hadn't had in that cold, brutal darkness. Pain, humiliation, horror. Those things rose bitter and vile in her throat, strangling her sobs the way that tape and wadding of cloth had muffled her screams. Her body convulsed, recalling every ruthless detail of what it had suffered in that black hollow of time that seemed to go on forever, that void of hope and helplessness from which her soul still recoiled, until finally, feebly at first and then with increasing intensity, it cried *Enough! Stop! I'm not that helpless, hopeless creature anymore! I survived and I will not go back to that place again!*

Then there was only the cooling jet of the water and the quiet after an emotional storm.

She remained cramped and huddling for a long, anxious moment, waiting for the rush of memories to return, but there was only a quiet whisper, a faint residue of fear. She took a cautious breath and then another, deeper one as the water continued to swirl down the drain. Gradually, she was able to stand, to turn off the shower and dry off as tremors of delayed shock and stress rippled through her. But she managed. Slowly, shakily, she managed. And within her, a seed of inner strength took root and began to grow with tenacity.

Clad in a hotel robe, her hair turbaned in a towel, Toni emerged from the bathroom to a darkened main area. The only light was from the swollen moon hanging low in the sky beyond their balcony.

Zach sat on the couch, motionless. Knowing what he'd

witnessed, that he now understood her degradation, she worried how he would react to her. With pity or repulsion? A cowardly part of her urged that she slink to her bed and burrow under covers of shame and isolation. But a strong voice spoke louder, demanding that she face her fears head on.

It was the longest walk of her life from the bathroom door to the couch where Zach sat impassive in his opinions. With anguish thickening in her throat, she forced a faint smile and a tone not quite as barren as her spirit.

"Not exactly my best work for television."

Odd emotions cramped his expression. When he looked up at her, unable to speak, she knew with an awful desolation that she'd lost him to the horror of a past he'd never be able to get over.

Then, as that paralyzing ache settled around her heart, Toni began to turn away.

His hand on her wrist stopped her.

She couldn't make herself look at him again. Her courage had fled. She couldn't face the knowing in his eyes now that he knew it all.

"Toni."

The compelling way he said her name coaxed her attention back to him.

In the darkness, his gaze glittered.

"You are the bravest woman I've ever known."

A choking sound escaped her as he gently pulled her down to him.

For a long while, he simply held her. From that strong, steady circle of support, Toni relinquished the burdens that scarred her soul. And only then did a near miraculous sense of self-forgiveness banish all traces of the guilt and shame she'd carried since that van pulled up beside a reckless teenager ten years ago. She sighed as his lips touched her brow. Then his next words threatened her newfound serenity.

"I'm afraid I'm going to have to ask for more of that courage from you."

Warned by the somber currents in his voice, Toni drew a deep breath to steel herself as she leaned away. "What could be worse than what you've just seen?"

"Telling me about it."

A lump of ice dropped to the pit of her belly. Seeing her distress, Zach cupped her cheek in his hand, his thumb riding the lush curves of her lips as they trembled slightly.

"What do you need to know?"

"Everything. Every detail you can remember from the afternoon when we…talked to the instant I pulled the tape from your eyes in that cellar. Everything. What you heard, what you smelled, what you felt."

"Okay." Her firm response belied the bleakness seeping into her system. *Everything.* She didn't know if she could be that brave.

"Toni, someone is out there capitalizing on your pain. Someone who knows just how to hurt you, who knows facts only someone on the inside could have. Someone who had your blouse and this tape and access to your fears. Until we find out who that is, they're not going to stop."

The enormity of that sank in deep and cold.

"Then we'll have to stop them, won't we, because I'm through living in fear. I am not going to let this thing hold me hostage any longer."

Zach nodded but his gaze reflected his pride in her. That

heat reached to places that hadn't known warmth for far too long.

"Start anywhere you feel comfortable."

"None of it makes me comfortable." Her laugh was rusty and raw. "But I guess I should start with a silly girl propositioning her bodyguard."

The telling of her tale went on into the early hours of the morning beginning with the kiss that almost happened and concluding with the warmth of his arms and the solidity of his promise. *I won't tell anyone. I swear upon my life.* Neither of them had guessed at the importance of those two events in the shaping of their futures until they heard them brought back to life in the quiet security of a Mexican hotel room a world away from the source of the original hurt. But somehow, that much closer to the original feelings ignited between them. In hearing the event played out again, moment by moment, emotion by emotion, they were also putting it behind them.

When she'd finished purging her memories and cleansing her soul, Toni was drained of all but a feeling of relief. It was over at last. The sense of closure she'd been denied when begging her secret not be told was finally granted as she sat with her head resting on his broad shoulder, with her words resting heavy upon his heart.

It should have been you.

Zach closed his eyes and absorbed the agony of that claim. All his anger, all his zealous insistence upon his rules, none of it meant a thing when compared to that soul-rendingly simple statement. Had he thought more of her heart than the rigid dictates of his duty, how different things might have been.

"It's time for you to put it behind you, Toni. I'll do whatever I can to help."

And if that meant closing him out because of the part he played in her misery, he would accept that in exchange for her chance at the normal life she craved.

How inadequate that sounded compared to what she'd endured but apparently, it was enough.

She lifted her head so she could meet his gaze. "I know you would. You've done too much already."

If he hadn't been lost in the drowning pools of her eyes, he might have heard the hint of dismissal in her words. But he was sinking fast and not fighting against the sensations as they closed over his head.

He sealed the moment with a tender kiss. To him, her response carried them from closing a chapter of the past to exploring new avenues for a potential future.

But waking not too many hours later in the tangled sheets of their lovers' bed, Zach felt his sense of satisfaction flee when one other fact came to the forefront.

He was wrong in his assumptions.

And he was alone in the room.

Antonia was gone.

Chapter 16

Toni and the crew were gone, had pulled out lock, stock and camera lens at dawn. He tried to contact Tomas on his cell, but the call wouldn't go through. No signal. At least she wasn't out there without any help available. Small consolation as his guilt kicked in.

Arrangements had to have been made to move so many so fast and only one name came to mind. Zach asked at the desk and, after slipping some extra pesos across the counter, was directed to the beach.

The ocean was restless, roaring to the sand with white caps and seething foam. A black flag had been posted once again to warn of treacherous waters. As treacherous as Zach's mood as he approached the thatched palapa. The occupant sprawled in a chaise still wore last night's clothing and dark glasses.

"Where's Toni and her crew?" Zach didn't bother with polite banter.

"If she wanted you to know, she would have told you," came the surly reply.

Having no patience with the sullen attitude, Zach gripped Mateo Chavez by the sloppy shirt and hauled him upright into a sagging seated position. "She's in danger, you fool. Tell me where she is."

He knocked back the sunglasses so he could effect some eye-to-eye intimidation.

Someone had apparently beaten him to the intimidation part. Literally.

Mateo blinked up at him through eyes swollen by drink and someone's enthusiastic fists. "You don't have to worry about Premiero bothering her. We've already talked. He knows the deal's off and there's no way Toni's going to change her mind about it. He's not happy but he's not homicidal, either."

"The sight of your face doesn't make a strong case for that, mate."

"That's because of a different matter."

"What had you promised him?"

Mateo laughed. The sound was as raw as his features. "Toni's compliance. He was going to forgive a rather large debt if I helped things go smoothly with the merger."

Zach was very close to adding a few contusions of his own to Mateo's colorful collection. "And how were you going to do that?" he growled. "By scaring her into submission?"

"What?" He looked comically blank for a moment, then his expression puckered with revulsion. "You mean with the video? I would never do anything to bring Antonia distress. I care more about her than my own worthless life."

"How were you planning to earn Premiero's forgiveness?"

"Silly me, I thought to romance her into being agreeable." He laughed in hindsight. "I'd forgotten how opinionated Toni can be on most any subject. But dear, sweet Toni. She offered me a loan instead of her affection. I guess we know where that was already engaged."

Zach scowled at the sourly spoken reference. "So you took her money."

Mateo gestured to his face. "Does it look like it? I've taken without remorse or regret from the two women who loved me all my life, letting them bail me out of every careless situation I've gotten myself into. This time, my pride would not allow it. I thought Premiero could be persuaded, mano a mano, to give me more time. But, as you see, he was not in the mood to be charitable." Mateo gave a helpless gesture. "No good deed goes unpunished." He glanced up at the soaring white tower, his expression bleak.

"I could have made something of this place. I had a real talent for it, you know. What a thing to discover that your ship has come in as it's sinking beneath you."

"You couldn't bring Toni to the negotiation table, so he's calling his loan?"

"That's about it. And that's all folks. I have no way to meet his demand. I'll have to sell. And he'll pick up the pieces for next to nothing and profit off all my hard work."

Zach regarded the young man whose first attempt at genuine chivalry had cost him all. And he was reminded of another who'd made a choice that had nearly ruined him. They had the same taste in headstrong women, so how could Zach abandon him?

"Perhaps not."

Mateo perked up cautiously.

"Perhaps another investor might be convinced to step in before Premiero starts breaking legs."

"Who would go against Premiero? I know no man with that kind of death wish."

"It's not a man. And it's time someone besides Toni told Premiero no."

"That would be the best news I've had this morning, other than waking up alive."

It probably was.

"Call Cecilia Roberts. Tell her I said she should listen to your proposal."

He could see the perplexity in the younger man's face, but Mateo Chavez was not one to let an opportunity pass. "I will." He nodded to himself then regarded Zach with a new directness. "Toni's gone into the jungle to get the zipline shots. She didn't feel there was any need to disturb you since Premiero is no longer a threat."

Zach's features tightened. "I need to know where they are, exactly."

"She'll be perfectly safe. I set her up with a reputable guide. Veta's with her. And Premiero's yacht left the marina this morning."

Zach's stance didn't loosen as he said, "Premiero wasn't the threat."

It was like riding straight down on a bullet train with your head out the window.

Toni cannonballed through the jungle canopy with knees tucked, her shriek of exhilaration trailing behind her. Greenery flashed by the way one's life would if this was a free fall. But Toni wasn't hurtling to a sudden death. She was flying toward a new life.

And she was loving every minute of it.

The morning's exhausting work was done. Bryce had his cavern shots of her rock climbing and rappelling. She looked great, he assured her. The shoes looked great. This was the final sequence for the campaign, this wild, free wheeling ride through the exotic scenery, rocketing into her future with abandon.

Nothing had ever given her such a rush, such a sensation of total satisfaction. Or so she thought until she was being unhooked from her harness and saw Zach Russell standing there.

His expression was compressed into a volatile thundercloud of disapproval but she didn't care. He'd just have to get over it. The way she'd gotten over all the baggage she'd been dragging behind her. The past was the past and the future was so bright she had to wear shades.

"Fabulous, darling. Just fabulous," Bryce cooed as he finished snapping off a few candids of her flushed face and dazzling smile. "We're done. It's Dom time."

"You've earned it. You all have. Aletta's going to the top with this campaign and you've made it happen."

Bryce fell uncharacteristically serious for a moment as he pinched her chin. "No, sweetie, you made it happen. Your mom would have been proud."

She was able to face Zach then, with tears of emotion still glistening in her eyes and adrenaline coursing hotly through her veins. Other feelings, hot, deep, desire-drenched feelings, swelled inside her as she adored the sight of his hawkishly handsome face. It took all her self-control not to launch herself right into his arms.

"Hi."

He didn't say anything. His granite expression said it all. He was royally peeved.

"Before you start beating me over the head with Rule Two, let me assure you that this wasn't some flighty stunt just to get your blood pressure up."

"You certainly succeeded in that."

She ignored his wry comment, desperately needing him to understand the cathartic revelation that came to her at dawn. As she sat looking down on his sleeping features, with her heart hammering hard and her vision so clear, she could see for miles. "I had to do this, Zach. No more hiding. No more seeking approval. I had to do it on my own. Without you, without my father, without Premiero. Just me taking responsibility for what my mother entrusted to me."

"Are you quite done?"

She heaved a massive sigh, not bothering to apologize. "Yes, I am."

"You're looking pleased with yourself."

She grinned. "Yes, I am."

"Good. Then let's go. I have only one responsibility and that's to get you safely on a plane tomorrow morning."

Her mood took a sudden sobering nosedive as reality kicked the slats out from under her success. "And then?"

"I'm taking a long vacation. Some place simple, without phones and with great sauce."

Would those plans include a companion, she wondered as she said her goodbyes to the crew and allowed herself to be loaded into his small rental car.

"Where's Tomas?" Zach asked as he motioned for her to buckle up.

"Veta needed to take a call from the States and Tomas

took her back to the hotel. We're going to all meet at Ban-
dido's in Zihua for drinks and Cuban cigars later this
morning. Then the guys are going golfing and the gals are
going to work on a strapless tan."

"Sounds like an eventful day."

"And you sound like you're about to throw a wet blanket on all of it."

He looked at her sitting there in the passenger seat, her
skin still flushed from the wild ride, her features relaxed
for the first time since he'd met her ten years ago. She
looked young and happy and free of shadows. And he
couldn't bring himself to cast them back over her. Not yet,
anyway.

"What kind of bodyguard would I be if I threw a blanket on a little nude sunbathing?"

Toni grinned. "That's the spirit."

Zach started the rental and, with Toni waving to her
crew, pulled out onto the road back to Ixtapa. And if they
came across a nice area for some nude sunbathing, he
wasn't opposed to pulling over and spreading out the blanket from the backseat for a little one on one celebration of
their own.

Pride in her and in what she'd accomplished created a
huge ache within his chest. What guts it must have taken
to pull a prize like Aletta out from under Premiero and in
doing so, defy the father who'd manipulated the family
strings so masterfully. It would have been easier to go
along, to accept the arranged path as inevitable and the role
of figurehead with good grace. But nothing about Antonia Castillo was made for the easy, uninvolved road. That
was the thing that frustrated him about her. And what he
loved about her.

What he loved about her.

Toni gave him a startled look as the car veered suddenly, bumping into the mounded shoulder and bouncing back onto the uneven pavement. "What? What's wrong? You look like you swallowed a bee."

A B-52 maybe.

"What?" He stared at her through equally startled eyes then blinked away the glaze of shock. "Nothing. I just realized there was something I forgot to do."

"What's that?"

"Something I'll have to take care of later."

He turned his attention back to the road and reluctantly, she decided not to pursue it.

He'd forgotten to tell her he was sorry. For her pain, for her fears, for the years of panic and uncertainty. For being such a coward, he couldn't admit now, even as he hadn't confessed then, to the feelings he had for her. Because if he did, if he dragged out all that emotional baggage, he'd lose the edge that made him valuable to her.

Right now she didn't need a lover. She needed a protector. And to be the best at what he did required the detachment that allowed him to do his job in her best interests, not his, despite her. So the blanket would remain in the backseat and his admission would remain unspoken. At least until the danger was past. And then…and then the topic would be open for discussion.

Some place simple, without phones and with great sauce.

The vehicle came out of nowhere.

The clear road behind him suddenly yielded a large, black diplomatic sedan with tinted windows riding right up on their bumper.

Zach cursed softly. "Hang on."

"What?" Toni twisted in the seat to look over her shoulder and that was when the sedan hit them. Hard. Intentionally. Whiplashing her in the confines of her seatbelt as Zach fought the wheel for control. "Who are they?" she cried in controlled alarm. "Premiero's men?"

"I'm not going to stop to ask them."

With that, Zach tromped down hard on the accelerator, sending the little car leaping forward to put some distance between them and the other vehicle. But the little six cylinder proved no match for whatever was under the hood of the sedan and it rapidly closed on them, looming up in the rearview with a menacing anonymity. The rental shuddered as it took another damaging hit to the rear. The trunk lid flew up, obscuring Zach's vision and before he was aware of it, the sedan edged around them, creeping up on the driver's side.

There was no way to get off the road. Jungle was on one side and a drainage culvert on the other. No witnesses or Samaritans were coming in either direction as the sedan slammed into the side of the compact, sending it, despite Zach's best efforts at the wheel, careening over the embankment on a jolting ride to the bottom of the runoff gully. There they came to an abrupt stop, the horn blaring and steam from under the crumpled hood escaping in an ominous cloud.

He didn't realize his head was bleeding until he had to wipe the blood away to see for himself that Toni was all right. She was unbuckling her seatbelt, turning to him in concern when the passenger door was yanked open.

"Zach!"

She disappeared out of the vehicle.

Grabbing for his gun, Zach pushed against his door and found it too damaged to open. He scrambled across the passenger seat, blinded by the hot crimson pouring down his face, blinded by the deep inner terror that he wasn't going to be able to prevent what was about to happen.

He could hear Toni's fierce epithets as she fought against those who held her. He half fell out the open door. A knee caught him in the cheekbone, driving him backward. He struggled to bring his gun into play as the car door swung shut on his hand. He heard his bones breaking through the hot roar of pain. His gun fell from numbed fingers.

"No, don't kill him!"

He heard Toni's shriek through the cresting rumble of unconsciousness surging up over him.

"Don't shoot. I'll sign the papers."

She didn't know where they were going. Toward a meeting with Premiero most likely. It didn't matter. What mattered was the blood soaking her cargo shorts from where she cradled Zach's head on her lap. She was too worried to feel fear for her own situation. At the moment, there was nothing she could do to change it.

The solid black panel separating front from back seat was closed but she knew two men sat up there. Men as hard faced and ruthless as the Hispanic pair that regarded her from the opposing seat in back. They held semiautomatic pistols and she didn't presume to think that they'd be reluctant to use them. They were professionals not common criminals. That gave her some degree of hope that negotiations would follow rather than a quick, brutal end. Or a slow, drawn-out and horrifying one.

Her legs were shaking. She couldn't stop them. Her hands were unsteady, too, as she tried to stem the flow from Zach's head wound with the corner of her shirt. She glanced up at the duo across from her.

"Do you have a handkerchief? *Pañuelos?*"

The men exchanged stony looks but one reached into his jacket and withdrew a plain cotton square. She took it gratefully.

"Are we going to meet with Premiero?"

This time her question met with no response. Sighing, she gave up the idea of communicating with her captors and concentrated on the injured man laid out on the seat beside her.

The bleeding was from a gash above his brow where he'd hit the window frame. Spectacular bruising had already begun beneath his left eye, and from cheekbone to jawline on the right side of his face. His right hand trailed down to the floor mat, distorted by swelling. What scared her the most was the fact that he hadn't returned to awareness.

Even as she considered that, he moaned softly and stirred on the wide leather seat. The two men opposite took firmer grips on their weapons. Professional courtesy, she assumed.

"Zach?" She bent down over him as his eyes blinked open. His stare was cloudy, disoriented.

"Where?" he muttered faintly.

"Going up the mountainside. I haven't been told our destination. No place we want to go, I'm sure. But I don't think they can be persuaded to take us back to Ixtapa, either. We'll have to go along for the ride."

She could feel him cautiously testing his resources,

gingerly flexing muscles and estimating his reserves under their hosts' watchful eyes. Their tension eased at his weak, whispery groan.

Fearing he was more seriously injured than she'd at first believed, Toni fought down her own panic to reassure him. It might not have been the smartest thing to let her captors know that she had feelings for him, feelings that could be used against her at some later time. She only thought in the moment. And she wanted Zach Russell to know what was in her heart in case she never had another opportunity to tell him.

She leaned over until her lips brushed his colorful cheek, so her whisper would reach his ear.

"Zach, I want you to know—"

"Rule Two."

She thought she misunderstood him. Rule Two?

Where you go, I go.

His knees suddenly tucked under him as he made an awful moaning sound.

"Zach?"

"I'm going to throw up."

His raspy claim got their escorts's attention. Alarmed at the thought of having to share the enclosed backseat with the aftermath of a bout of sickness, they looked to each other in confused distress.

"Get them to slow down. Open the door. Do it."

Toni's urgent command had one of them punching the intercom, requesting that the vehicle slow. While Zach made desperate wretching noises, the guard leaned forward to unlatch and lift the door handle.

And that's when Zach exploded in motion.

The steel toe of his boot caught the second man in the

temple, knocking him into the first who was already off balance. Zach's elbow swung in a tight arc, connecting with his chin.

The door swung wide. The jungle flew past, offering a blur of escape.

"Go!"

When she didn't respond to Zach's order quickly enough, he shoved her hard through the opening, snagging one of their dazed assailant's guns before hurtling after her.

The car had still been moving around thirty miles per hour. Toni hit the shoulder of the road with a spine-jarring force. Her senses swam and the world went momentarily dark. She felt Zach's arms lock around her and then they were airborne. The sensation of flight lasted all too briefly. They hit the ground hard, taking a bounce then rolling, tumbling wildly down the steep mountainside.

The drop seemed to go forever. Over the snapping of the brush as they tore through it, she could hear the staccato of weapon fire but they plunged too quickly out of sight for any of the bullets to find a target. Finally, she smacked into a tree trunk with her shoulder, the impact slowing their descent, but sending a shock of agony coursing through her.

For a moment, she lay on the damp jungle floor with the green canopy circling above her in great, sickening loops until her senses began to steady.

"Are you all right?"

She tried to nod in answer to Zach's curt question but her neck wouldn't move. "I feel like I've been thrown from a moving car."

"Up. We've got to go."

The idea of actually getting to her feet was so ridiculous, Toni had to pinch her lips together to keep laughter from escaping.

But Zach, she discovered, was deadly serious.

He grabbed her arm, dragging her up to a wobbly stance. The scenery whirled and swooped for a few dizzying seconds, then Zach was dragging her after him through the close stand of trees, anxious to distance them from any potential pursuit.

They ran with no destination in mind except escape. Heat steamed up through the dense foliage until they were dripping from the heavy weight of humidity. Zach's grip on her arm never lessened and it was keep pace or be towed beside him. She ran, stumbling, wheezing, hurting, but too motivated to protest. The sound of gunfire still echoed in her recent memory. If they were caught, she didn't think their captors would be so kind as to keep Zach alive no matter how much she tried to bargain. They were running for their lives, and losing Zach before she had a chance to finish telling him what she'd started to say in the car was not an option.

They burst from the tangled forest into ordered rows of fruit trees. Sunlight glared down through the branches in streaks of hazy brightness, dazzling their eyes and blinding them to the approach of a vehicle until it was nearly upon them.

Zach pointed the pistol at the windshield and shouted for the vehicle to stop. His head was pounding. His hand throbbed in fierce pulse beats that battered at the last stronghold of his awareness. By shading his eyes with his mangled hand, he could make out an old rusty pickup with a family of farmers in the back. They stood frozen at the sight of the weapon. He took a chance and lowered it.

"Can you help us? *Puede usted ayudarme, por favor?*"

An ancient man in a torn straw cowboy hat climbed out of the truck's cab and cautiously drew closer.

"What you need?" he asked in broken English.

"A cell phone."

When he looked perplexed, Zach gestured with thumb and little finger at his ear and mouth. The farmer shrugged and shook his head. No help there.

"Can you give us a lift…a ride into Zihua?"

The man looked between the two of them, gauging their bedraggled and desperate appearance, an appearance that spoke of money nonetheless.

"Gas costs much. We would miss work."

"*Quanto?* How much do you want?" His vision began to waver, images rippling like a mirage in front of him. He didn't have time to barter.

An equally aged woman got out of the passenger side of the truck to stand behind her husband. She whispered something to him and pointed at Zach's wrist. Zach stripped off his watch without hesitation, eager to strike an agreeable bargain. The old woman took it and examined the metal with a practiced scrutiny. She nodded then stared at him more closely. She gestured to her own wrinkled earlobe.

His father's diamond. The symbol of everything that gave his life order and purpose. Then he glanced at Toni, seeing her through the increasing fog filling his head. Gorgeous, gutsy Antonia Castillo. And the sacrifice seemed inconsequential.

He passed his weapon to Toni and pulled the stud from his ear. As he reached out to hand it to the old lady, momentum carried him forward, dropping him to his knees.

Through the roaring in his head, he heard Toni calling his name. He struggled to stay conscious long enough to tell her the name of Tomas's family in Zihuatanejo. Then there were only snatches of awareness. The straw-littered bed of a truck jouncing down a grassy lane. The flicker of the sun peekabooing through tree branches. The sounds of traffic, of Toni's soothing voice speaking words he couldn't comprehend. And then the rough, bumpy ride that woke exquisite torment as they wove up the cliffside tracks to a home in the mountains.

He lost it then. The next sound he heard was a familiar deep-throated rumble over a vibration that jarred his aching head. He managed to open his eyes long enough to recognize the interior of a military transport plane and the swarthy features of his best friend bending near.

"Toni?" he croaked out.

"Safe," Jack Chaney told him. "I see I'll have to do more stitching."

Zach tried to smile, but that small effort was enough to carry him into a deep blackness in which he finally found relief.

Chapter 17

He opened his eyes to familiar ceiling frescoes.

His apartment?

Zach lifted his hand to test the enormous ache in his head, only to be distracted by the bulky wrappings that extended from fingertips to mid-forearm.

"Welcome back."

Zach moved his eyes—because moving his head was out of the question—to his left where Jack Chaney had drawn up a chair and made himself comfortable.

His first attempt at speech was a low rasp. He wet his lips and tried again. "How long?"

"Going on day five. You've got a whopper of a concussion. It took some fancy string pulling to keep you out of the hospital. I knew you wouldn't be able to stomach the food."

"Thanks for that."

Jack grinned. "You're welcome."

He gestured with his half-cast. "What's the story here?"

"Not a happily-ever-after, I'm afraid. You managed to shatter about every bone in there. The doctor wouldn't even hazzard a guess about recovery of use until after you finish a rather grueling bout of physical therapy."

Zach took a slow breath before asking, "Bottom line?"

"You'll have to find another line of work."

He took a moment to absorb that, then looked to his friend. "Well, you don't seem broken up by my misfortune."

"Sometimes we need a wake-up call to tell us it's time to move on. Well, it's time, my friend."

Zach sighed philosophically. His lack of resistance to the idea surprised him. Maybe it was the drugs. Maybe not. "I had a good run."

"Yes, you did."

Then his attention sharpened. "But I also had unfinished business."

"She's out in your greenhouse, so relax. We've got some talking to do before you see her."

Warned by the somber nature of his friend's reply, Zach refused to hear the news flat on his back like an invalid. He struggled to sit up, with Jack meeting him halfway with a bolster of pillows.

"So talk."

"I had a buddy in forensics run that bloodstain on the blouse from the kidnapping and type the DNA from the piece of fabric found after the attack at the house."

Zach couldn't believe their luck. "And they matched?"

"No. Not quite."

"Not quite? That's like being almost pregnant. It either

matches or it doesn't." He wasn't in the mood for games. His head ached, making mental gymnastics a painful impossibility. If not for the wrapping on his hand, he might have considered strangling his friend.

"Unless they're related."

All thoughts of choking Jack Chaney fled.

"Who are we talking about?"

He listened to Jack lay it out on a time line. And it made sense. An awful, coldly calculating sense.

But how was he going to tell Toni?

After the tropical warmth in Mexico, February's frigid greys held no welcome. But in Zach Russell's rooftop garden, spring was already in flower. Even the weakest sunshine created warmth through the angled glass roof. The profusion of delicate orchids was a surprise but not the pungent utilitarian purpose of the majority of what was grown. Herbs, fresh and abundant, were everywhere, filling pots in the iron baker's racks lining the walls, thriving in the raised central garden where a fountain gurgled a restful melody. Toni was content to just relax in the cushioned chaise and soak up the aromatic ambiance, or would have been if her thoughts weren't focused inside the sprawling rooms, on the man recovering there.

The past few days had flown by in a blur of unexpected events. When Tomas arrived in answer to a call from his family's humble home, it was with a military escort. She and Zach were whisked to an extremely well guarded airstrip where a flight awaited. The station was manned by a hard-featured multinational force who didn't look receptive to questions. So she didn't ask any. Once they were Stateside, Zach was wheeled into an emergency room and she was met during her agonizing wait by Jack Chaney. She was afraid she didn't make a very good impression on him. He suggested, politely, that she go with him to Chicago. She told him, not so nicely, to go to hell. She wasn't leaving Zach Russell's side.

And so here she was, in Zach's European home, in the world away from his work that he'd created as a respite from the ugliness of what he did. Being here filled in the rest of the blanks of what she knew of Zach. He was wealthy, he was cultured, he had a deep, nurturing side denied expression except in this verdant setting. He lived two separate lives, one of privilege and genteel intellectual pursuits and one of a dark and deadly nature that brought international intrigue hand-in-hand with death regularly to his door. He had a closet full of Italian suits and an opera collection. And enough weapons to arm a Third World coup.

Which one had she fallen in love with? The philanthropist or the warrior?

"That rather scraggly looking fellow over there makes a wonderful healing tea. I think we could both benefit from it, since we look as though we survived a small urban war."

Delight in seeing Zach up and about conflicted with Toni's sudden awareness of how she must look. She hadn't had time to shop and her bloodstained clothing was beyond repair. Jack had found her a pair of Zach's sweatpants and a baggy T-shirt. With her hair pulled back in a simple ponytail and her scratched face bereft of makeup, she could probably pass for a bag lady. Zach, on the other hand, oddly benefitted from the trials he'd endured. The stitches, the bruising, the bandages created a heroic aura about him. He'd earned the battle scars protecting her life and that knowledge stirred a heat deep in her belly that no herbal tea could rival.

"Should you be out of bed?" She couldn't control the tug of anxiousness pulling at the edge of that question.

"Don't concern yourself, love. I assure you that I feel worse than I look."

His faint, lopsided smile had her emotions doing somersaults, then his next words knocked her completely off balance.

"You'll be leaving for the airport with Jack in twenty minutes." He put up his splinted hand to stave off the anticipated protests. "You have to go. A claim has already been made against the insurance policy you took out in the event of a kidnapping. If you don't show up to throw a monkey wrench into the deal, my guess is your company will be in Premiero's pocket by this time tomorrow."

"How?"

"Your father has power of attorney, does he not?"

Toni fell silent, mulling over the circumstances that would naturally follow her disappearance. They'd assume the worst. They'd pay whomever demanded it of them and when she wasn't returned, she'd be presumed dead. If she didn't put a quick end to that rumor, there was a good chance someone would try to make the supposition into fact.

"Premiero's plane touches down at O'Hare tomorrow at two. My guess is he'll be on the way to your front door as soon as he clears customs."

One thing had always bothered her and she spoke it now. "Why is he so set on this merger with Aletta? He has other investments worth far more."

"It's not the company. It's his way into doing business legitimately in the States and widening his base abroad. And more than that, it's personal. It's the chance to control your father."

"And he'd kill me to do that?" Her stark tone reflected her inner horror.

"These men don't play by the rules of morality or honor. They play for stakes of pride and power. They'd sacrifice family, freedom, their fortunes, anything. And you still have what they want."

"Well, it's not theirs to fight over."

"It will be if you're not on that plane." His voice softened. "Jack will take good care of you."

Her panicked objections surged. He wasn't going with them. "I don't want Jack to take care of me. You're the only one I trust."

He made a helpless gesture with his shattered hand. "Sorry, darling. I'm not much good to you now."

He was pushing her away, out of his life, out of his future. And she couldn't let it happen. Not like this.

Toni went to where he was standing, a saving grace apart, just inside the doorway. He stiffened incrementally at her approach but she couldn't let that matter.

"Zach, I'm sure Mr. Chaney is a good man. But it's you I want."

"You'll have to take what you can get, Toni, and be satisfied. I can't help you. I can't even help myself." If that fact angered or frustrated him, he hid it well behind the flat tone and flatter expression.

She reached up to touch his battered cheek. He'd gone so still, she didn't think he was breathing.

"I need you."

He never so much as blinked at her impassioned plea. He caught her wrist gently, firmly, with his good hand and drew her arm down. His response was as coldly separating as a plasma cutter.

"No, you don't. Not anymore. You're strong enough to tackle anything, Toni. You proved that when you stood up to Premiero, when you faced down those abductors without flinching. You can handle your own future, love. You know you can. You don't need me."

"Maybe need was the wrong word."

She kissed him. Fiercely, frantically, with open mouth and open heart, trying to force him by his own response to deny everything he'd just said to her. He allowed the exchange, even participated to a slight degree but when the fire failed to catch and his lips remained cool, she stood down and backed away. He regarded her through expressionless eyes.

"Rule Three," he told her with heartbreaking simplicity. "Never get involved with the job."

She returned his stoic stare so he'd never know how those words devastated her. "I just figured out that some rules are there for a reason."

And she walked away from him without a goodbye.

An hour later, she was over the Atlantic, her face turned to the bulkhead pretending to sleep so Jack wouldn't know she was crying.

They were seated in the living room, old friends, old nemeses. The thing that struck Toni the hardest was not the shock in her father's face, but the fleeting instant of disappointment as he saw her standing there in Zach Russell's shapeless clothing. Alive.

"I'm sorry. Am I interrupting something?"

Quickly recovering himself, Victor Castillo started to stand, his arms opening for an embrace.

"Antonia! You cannot imagine my surprise."

"Oh, I think I can," came her wry retort. "Please don't get up. There's no need."

He dropped back into his chair, frowning at her disrespectful tone. Across from him, Premiero regarded her with the same black, indiscriminately ruthless eyes as those of the crocodile in the marina. She didn't try to disguise the disdain in her voice or the dislike from her expression.

"You wasted no time hurrying to convey your condolences to my poor prematurely bereaved father."

"You cannot know, dear Antonia, how happy I am to see that we were wrong."

She smirked at his slickly delivered speech. "Oh, I'm sure. That's why you just happen to have the paperwork for the Aletta merger with you, just in case my father could put aside his grief long enough to take care of some unfinished business. How rude of me to show up alive to ruin this touching moment."

"Antonia, you are obviously too distressed by your recent ordeal to know what you are saying."

"I am distressed, Father. Do you know why? Because you sit there with my mother's company ready to do business with the man who would collect on my kidnapping insurance policy. And that you are more upset by my rudeness than your friend's willingness to make a profit off my supposedly dead body."

The fact that he didn't try to deny it, that he didn't even have the good grace to look embarrassed by it, cut Toni's heart to shreds. This was the man she'd admired. That she'd tried so hard to please.

To Premiero, she said coldly, "Sorry you made the flight for nothing. Have a pleasant trip back."

"Antonia," Victor began in a tone that would allow no argument, "he's not leaving until our business is concluded."

"And what business is that? Extortion? Blackmail? What exactly, Father? What would mean more to you than your daughter's life?" Her laugh was harsh. "Oh, I forgot. You don't place much value there, do you? It's always been about your fortune, the fortune you made off my mother and now think you can control through me." Her tone hardened. "Think again."

Victor took a deep, furious breath, his features reddening with insult and aggravation. "You will not speak to me with that tone. I am the man of this house and you will do what you are told. You will sign these papers because it's what's best for the family."

"The family?" She laughed long and loud. "Since when has this been a loving family? If you wanted family, you could have had my affection and my loyalty. All you had to do was pay the price for it. Then I wouldn't think of going against your wishes now. I never would have thought to doubt your intentions. But if you think you can hold my life so cheaply then demand *my* company, you are wrong and ten years too late."

"You forget your place."

"Like my mother used to?"

Victor's glare was murderous. He chose to ignore her comparison. "If you dare discredit me and my word by breaking this deal, I will disown you."

"There's only one man I know whose word I would take at face value, and as for cutting me out of your heart and home, you did that a long time ago."

Emotions churning, tears warring for release, Toni had to look away from the two heartless schemers. She stared out at the icy water of Lake Michigan and tried to draw strength from the sight of the relentless waves battering against a barricaded shore. That's how she'd felt trying to win her father's respect and devotion. No matter how long or how hard she pushed against it, she couldn't wear down the barriers he built around him and his money.

She swiped at her eyes, refusing to display weakness now. In a moment she would walk out of the house she'd been raised in, away from the father she'd been taught to revere, from a heritage she'd been trained to uphold. All she had to do was find the inner strength to take that first step.

A glint on the snow-covered hillside near the caretaker's summer cottage caught her eye. A reflection of some sort. She studied it for a moment, puzzled then suddenly shocked into immobility by the realization of what it was.

It was the flash from an assassin's rifle scope.

She was pressing the panic button on her bracelet even before she remembered. There was no one to hear as she called for Zach Russell as glass exploded all around them.

Chapter 18

It was bitterly cold, but the wait was worthwhile as Antonia Castillo finally came into the high powered rifle's cross hairs. Just a squeeze of the trigger and it would be done. Balance would again be restored to a plan set in motion ten years ago.

Finger tightening on the trigger, Veta Chavez allowed a small smile of satisfaction. It froze on her face as the unmistakable bore of a pistol barrel pressed beneath her ear.

"Moving wouldn't be a good idea," Zach Russell told her with a crisp factuality she didn't doubt for an instant. She lowered the rifle and made her hands visible.

"Are you sure you want to do this to Toni?"

"Believe me," Zach drawled. "I think she'd take the news of your betrayal better than a bullet to the brain."

"You don't know the whole of it."

"Enough to know that all you had to do was continue

to play the best friend. No one would have suspected you had any part in that kidnapping ten years ago. But your greed just couldn't let it go."

"Don't you even want to know why?"

She was stalling for time but Zach couldn't resist the bait. "Why?"

"He killed my mother. That car crash was no accident. He found out his wife was going to leave him and was afraid all her lovely money was going with her. My mother wasn't even supposed to be in that car. She was driving because Mercedes Castillo was too upset to get behind the wheel. He killed my mother and I'm going to make sure everything that was once his is mine." She turned slowly to bestow an icy smile upon him. "A family trait passed father to daughter. Now my father and I will have all that was once his and his daughter's."

"There's one other piece of information you should know."

Veta's eyes narrowed. "What's that?"

"Before you go blaming everything on Victor Castillo, you might want to consider who he paid to arrange for that accident. And you might want to ask him why the fact that your mother was in that car didn't stop him from carrying out his plan."

There was no flicker of expression to warn him of what she meant to do. She just reacted. She swung the rifle butt sharply upward so that it clipped his injured hand. A mind-blanking pain shut down his awareness of all but the beep from Toni's bracelet. Just long enough for her to whirl and get off a single shot.

The sound echoed to Zach's soul as he brought Veta Chavez down to her knees while speaking into his two-way.

"Jack, shot fired. Where are you?"

"Coming up behind you. Anyone hit?"

"I don't know."

That admission scored his heart like a hot knife as he looked up toward the shattered window of the Castillo home.

The first thing he saw was blood pooling on the hardwood floor.

One of the full-length windows had been blown out by the shot. Glass was everywhere. The bitter cold from off the lake intruded into the house. When he saw Angel Premiero collapsed back on his chair with his hand clasped to an oozing shoulder, Zach's gush of relief plumed in the air.

Toni was standing off to the side, shock then relief filling her expression. She didn't come to him, because just then Jack and Tomas marched a cuffed Veta Chavez into the living room.

"Veta?"

The woman laughed, a remorseless sound. Her features were a caricature of the companion Toni had known and loved so well. "So surprised. How are you going to lead an international company when you can't tell friend from foe? It was going to be mine, Toni. My father promised." Then she glared at Premiero. "But it would seem that you're not the only one who's been deceived by fancy words and false deeds."

"Your father?" That came from a stunned Victor Castillo who stopped brushing shards of glass out of his hair long enough to cast an amazed look between father and daughter.

"He wanted someone he could trust close to you. That he could trust, like you were supposed to be able to trust Antonia. But she ruined everything, didn't she? After all you gave her, she turned on you. Just like your wife. She wouldn't behave, either, would she? That's why you arranged for her accident."

"What?" Toni looked to her father, begging to be told it wasn't true. But even before he spoke his denials, she could see it in his eyes, the guilt, the shame. And the anger that he'd been found out.

Victor stopped trying to cover his tracks, because there was more at risk than the auto accident. He glared at Veta, willing her silent. "You are condemning yourself, foolish girl."

"What do I care?" Her laugh was brittle this time, dancing on the edge of hysteria. "I'm tired of this little family game of intrigue. The only thing I care about is that my brother not suffer for what's discovered here today. He's the only one who is innocent of any wrongdoing. The rest of us deserve what we get, but not him."

"Keep talking. I'll do my best to see he's not brought into it."

Veta spared Zach a grateful look. Then the venom returned. "Victor was more than happy at first to loan him the money to invest in the resort. But then as time passed, he started to feel less generous and began to question the value of the secrets I was keeping for him. Such ugly, ugly secrets."

"You had my mother killed." The pain in Toni's voice was a palpable thing as she tried to absorb the awful truth.

"It was business with your mother. Always business. I couldn't let her go. She would have taken everything I worked to build between us."

Veta chuckled. "She found out about the money you were paying every month to keep my father quiet about your past in Mexico. You were siphoning it out of the company through a different set of books. That's why Aletta's real difficulties never surfaced until recently. You were able to cover them up until you'd almost bled it dry. She didn't like that, did she? She was saving the company as her daughter's nest egg. And you couldn't stand that, could you? That she would give it to a daughter instead of her husband."

"It should have been mine," Victor snarled. "She had no right shutting me out. I needed those funds. I had debts to pay."

"So you arranged for your precious daughter to be kidnapped and who better to call to handle it than your old friend from Mexico?"

All color drained from Toni's face. She gripped the back of a decorative chair because her knees threatened to give out on her. "I don't understand."

"You were never supposed to be in any danger." Castillo's promise was as empty as his affection. "It was for the money. But they wouldn't give it to me. Your bitch mother had built in safeguards with the company so I wouldn't have access under any circumstances. They wouldn't release the funds to me."

He hadn't not paid because he didn't want to. Rather because he couldn't. Toni struggled to breathe as her mind whirled about this new information.

Zach crossed the room to lift Premiero's unbloodied hand. Evidence of Toni's struggle to free herself was still scored deeply around his thumb. He glared up at Zach, his black eyes steeped in haughty fury and pain.

"Why?"

Premiero frowned slightly. "Why, what?"

"Why, when he couldn't get the money, didn't you just let her go unharmed?"

"You just can't get good help sometimes," was his matter-of-fact response.

"It was Steve," Veta spat out. "He wanted her. I told him it was just business, just for the money. But when the money didn't come through, he decided to take payment another way. I told him to stick to the plan, but he just couldn't keep his hands off her."

"So you killed him."

She smiled frostily at Zach's summation. "It seemed like a good idea at the time. He'd become a liability. A smart move, actually, considering how grateful the Castillos were for me killing that nasty bad man."

"Dead men tell no tales."

"But something did. What was it?" She had to know what had given her away.

"The blood on Toni's blouse. It had certain similarities to samples taken from a piece of material you left behind after you tried to frighten Toni by choking her with the necklace. Your DNA didn't match your supposed father's and that got me curious. I thought it might lead to Castillo but when it didn't, my friend Jack suggested another direction."

"How clever of you."

"That's what tripped you up. You were trying to be too clever. You wanted to see Toni and her father squirm. If you'd kept it simple instead of making it personal, you might have gotten away with it."

Veta smirked. "I told him not to hire you. I warned him

that it would be a mistake. But he thought you were a screw up, that your passion for his daughter would cloud your judgment like it did ten years ago. He thought bringing you in would put up a nice false front to keep Toni from becoming suspicious. All she had to do was go in the direction she was supposed to, toward signing the papers in Mexico. I tried to steer her in the right direction, but she wouldn't go. And when she wouldn't, my job was to push her, harder and harder, so that if she wouldn't sign, Victor could claim she was incompetent and take Aletta from her. If she'd been smart, she would have married my brother."

"And let you have the company through him?"

"Why not? I was going to get it anyway. Once the papers were signed. My father promised that the payment for all my hard work would be control of Aletta."

"But you were afraid he was lying, even then, weren't you?" Zach goaded.

"You convinced me to go to that club in London. That business in Colorado?" Toni's question was barely audible. "Was that you, too?"

"I arranged for the car accident," Veta gloated. "I took your precious ring, the one your mother gave you, the one the first kidnapper sent to your father as evidence that they had you. I needed the money to pay off Mateo's debt so he could be out from under your father's thumb. But, no big surprise, Victor wouldn't come up with the cash. I got just enough to keep him afloat, but it wasn't enough for him to become the success I knew he could be. That's when I approached my father and offered to do a little work on the side to make sure you were frightened enough to do anything they suggested."

"You were playing both sides, being clever," Toni added quietly.

"And why not? Why not do whatever I had to to see my brother and I were taken care of?"

"I would have seen to that, Veta," Toni told her, her heartbreak evident in her gaze, in her voice. "You, you and Mateo, were my family."

"Poor relations. We didn't want your charity, little rich girl. And if you had just cooperated, we wouldn't have needed it."

"So you set up my abduction on the road to collect the insurance for…"

"For your father, stupid. He had me suggest that policy to you through my brother as a backup, so he could claim the money to pay off his debt to my father in case the deal fell through. He was trying to cover all bases, but he didn't expect you to hit it over the wall and run."

"That's when you decided to pinch hit," Zach concluded. "You figured with Toni dead, Victor would sign the merger and you'd lead that happy little rich-girl life you always envied."

Veta shrugged. "It almost worked. It would have worked if they'd listened to me. I told them you were dangerous, that you were a professional who wouldn't be led around by his…baser instincts. I know men and I knew you'd be trouble."

"I'm bleeding to death here," Premiero grumbled. "Where's my ambulance and my lawyer?"

"On their way," Tomas promised. He stepped in to grip the mobster by his good arm. "Let's meet them outside, shall we?"

As he was led past his daughter, Veta spat at him, snarling, "You were supposed to take care of us."

"I would have, my dear. I would have. And before you

confess to anything else, you might remember that I still may. You won't need an ambulance or a lawyer. You'll need a mortician."

And that deadly vow finally silenced her.

"Time to go, Miss Chavez."

She balked at Jack's attempt to steer her toward the door and the multitude of police cars gathering there in the drive. She looked to Zach, her expression humbled as she asked, "You will keep your word about taking care of my brother?"

At his brief nod, she consented to go, heading toward a future she hadn't expected but well deserved.

And that left Victor Castillo.

Though her whole world was shaken to its foundation at discovering what kind of man her father really was, Toni had one final question, one that quavered with tenuous emotion.

"Why didn't you just tell me why you needed the money?"

He stared at her, his features all prideful arrogance. "A man does not ask for help from a woman."

"He does if he's a smart man," Zach concluded. He waved to the officers who were waiting for his signal. "Take him. Book him. Conspiracy, murder, fraud, kidnapping, for being a cold, heartless bastard and whatever else you can think of."

Castillo went quietly, with false dignity, never offering further explanation or apology to the daughter he'd wronged at every turn.

And then they were alone in the shattered remainders of Toni's dreams.

Zach watched her closely, not certain how she was

going to react to the enormity of what she'd learned. Would she fold in devastation? She had every right to. He was ready to step in, to wrap her up in his arms, to hold her until her innate balance was restored. But this was Antonia Castillo, not any other woman who'd just had her emotional legs cut out from under her. And she'd agreed with him in France that she didn't need him.

She took a slow, unsteady breath and released it in a forceful stream. She glanced at the fragmented window and the stains covering the chair and parquet floor.

"I need to get this taken care of before things get ruined." She considered her words then laughed softly. "As if they could get any worse."

Her shoulders trembled and Zach prepared to move in with the offer of his own. The sacrifice wasn't necessary. She recovered on her own to regard him with a sad yet sincere smile.

"Thank you for keeping your word to me, Zach, for being there when I needed you." She tapped the bracelet. "Thanks for being there when I called. It was a job well done. You proved my father wrong."

"It wasn't a job, Toni. I already had a job. It was a debt that needed paying. I never told you how sorry I was for what happened."

And she wasn't about to let him tell her now. "Consider it paid. You're free to go. Have Jack send me the bill."

"Rule Two," Zach reminded her.

Her brow knit in confusion.

"Where you go," he told her, "I go."

"Which means what, exactly?" Her heart had begun beating in a hurried, hopeful beat but she didn't dare, not yet, voice her deepest desire. That he meant what he was saying.

"I need a new line of work. I figure trying to keep up with you will provide me with all the excitement I'll ever need."

"You want to work for me?" She tried not to convey the magnitude of her disappointment. "As what? My bodyguard?"

"I'd consider that a perk, not a job duty. I was thinking of something a little more full-time with better benefits. I might just take my mother up on her offer as CEO so she can retire to something she's wanted to be for a long, long time. That's a retirement package I'll enjoy putting together for her." His eyes grew heavy lidded with speculation and heat raced through Toni from head to toe.

"And this will involve me, how?" she prompted, ready to engage in negotiations for the future she'd desired more than any of her many successes.

"On every level, lovey," was his smoldering promise. "From bedroom to boardroom. And if we're bored, we can get naked and roll around in all our combined assets."

"Just how much are you worth, Russell?"

"Not as much as you are to me."

That was the deal clincher she was looking for as she went gladly into his arms.

After a long, stock-taking kiss, she leaned back to observe him saucily. "If you're willing to throw out Rule One and Three, I promise to spend the rest of my life working on Rule Two."

"I have a better idea."

She traced the shape of his mouth with the tip of her tongue before asking, "And what would that be?"

"Let's just damn the rules and wing it."

"I'm right behind you on that one."

"No," he corrected with a soul-searing tenderness. "Not behind me. Beside me."

"Done," she murmured through the sudden fullness in her chest. She reached up for his lips.

Deal closed, it was time to celebrate the prospect of a long and prosperous merger.

* * * * *

Coming in September 2005 from

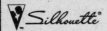

INTIMATE MOMENTS™

Hard Case Cowboy

by award-winning author

NINA BRUHNS

After a lifetime of bad luck, Redhawk Jackson had
finally hit the jackpot, working as the ranch foreman
on Irish Heaven. But when his boss's beautiful niece
shows up expecting to inherit his beloved ranch,
Hawk must decide what's most important—
his life's work or the woman of his dreams....

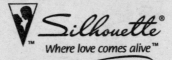

Where love comes alive™

COLLECTION

**From three favorite
Silhouette Books authors…**

CorNeReD

Three mystery-filled romantic stories!

Linda Turner

Ingrid Weaver

Julie Miller

Murder, mystery and mayhem are common ground
for three female sleuths in this short-story collection
that will keep you guessing!

On sale September 2005

Bonus Features:

**Author Interviews,
Author's Journal
Sneak Peek**

SCC

If you enjoyed what you just read,
then we've got an offer you can't resist!

Take 2 bestselling
love stories FREE!

Plus get a FREE surprise gift!

Silhouette®

COMING NEXT MONTH

INTIMATE MOMENTS®

#1383 LIVING ON THE EDGE—Susan Mallery
Bodyguard Tanner Keane expected his assignment to rescue a kidnapped heiress to be a no-brainer. And yet Madison Hilliard wasn't at all what he expected. As passion sparked between them, it was clear that his offer to keep her safe was anything but. Would their combustible attraction stand in the way of bringing down a deadly enemy?

#1384 PERFECT ASSASSIN—Wendy Rosnau
Spy Games
Her father was an assassin and after his murder, Prisca Reznik took on a target list of her own for revenge. On her mission, she encountered the very sexy Special Agent Jacy "Moon" Maddox, who was responsible for her father's capture. Could the man she meant to kill be the only man who could save her?

#1385 HARD CASE COWBOY—Nina Bruhns
No one ran faster from love than ranch foreman Redhawk Jackson, until Rhiannon O'Bronach, his benefactor's niece, arrived and made working together a necessity—and a sweet torture he'd never envisioned. As they ran the ranch and dealt with its hardships, Redhawk began to wonder if this tough-as-nails woman was a threat to his future...or the key to his happiness.

#1386 WHISPERS AND LIES—Diane Pershing
Investigative journalist Will Jamison was sniffing out a story that led him to an old friend. But little did he know the mystery of veterinarian Louise "Lou" McAndrew's past would draw him closer to her in every way. Not only had he stumbled upon a secret that involved a powerful politician, but Lou's strength and beauty made him rethink his vow to remain unattached. Could he love her and keep her out of harm's way?